D1743113

1 MONTH OF
FREE
READING

at

www.ForgottenBooks.com

By purchasing this book you are eligible for one month membership to ForgottenBooks.com, giving you unlimited access to our entire collection of over 1,000,000 titles via our web site and mobile apps.

To claim your free month visit:

www.forgottenbooks.com/free754039

* Offer is valid for 45 days from date of purchase. Terms and conditions apply.

ISBN 978-0-483-79140-4
PIBN 10754039

This book is a reproduction of an important historical work. Forgotten Books uses
state-of-the-art technology to digitally reconstruct the work, preserving the original format
whilst repairing imperfections present in the aged copy. In rare cases, an imperfection in
the original, such as a blemish or missing page, may be replicated in our edition. We do,
however, repair the vast majority of imperfections successfully; any imperfections that
remain are intentionally left to preserve the state of such historical works.

Forgotten Books is a registered trademark of FB &c Ltd.
Copyright © 2018 FB &c Ltd.
FB &c Ltd, Dalton House, 60 Windsor Avenue, London, SW19 2RR.
Company number 08720141. Registered in England and Wales.

For support please visit www.forgottenbooks.com

THE OLD LOVE IS THE NEW.

A Novel.

BY

MAURICE WILTON.

IN THREE VOLUMES.
VOL. III

London:

SAMUEL TINSLEY & CO.,
31, SOUTHAMPTON STREET, STRAND.
1880.

[*All Rights Reserved.*]

823
W711 o
v.3

CONTENTS OF VOL. III.

THE OLD LOVE IS THE NEW.

CHAPTER I.

THE EVE OF THE WEDDING.—SCENE II.

'Ah, why
With cypress branches hast thou wreathed thy bowers
And made thy best interpreter a sigh?
As those who dote on odours pluck the flowers
And place them on their breast—but place to die.'

WHEN Hugh arrived at Clonmore, he found Mr. Clavering waiting to receive him in the library.

There was no hearty welcome for him;

it was a formal business meeting, and Mr. Clavering was, as he sometimes could well be, repellent in manner and distant in his reserve. All the same, he intended to be present at Kathleen's wedding; but then he was going for her sake, or rather for the sake of his late friend, her father. Hugh Unyan was out of the question; he was a brother of Lady O'Moore's and the rival of Frank, and that was enough for Mr. Clavering.

The blind boy was sitting with the owner of Clonmore as Hugh entered the library.

It was a chilly evening, and a bright peat fire burnt in the grate. Pat sat beside it, and as the intruder entered, the boy ceased playing. Hugh had heard the last strains of the music as he was coming towards the door of the room.

The servant announced Mr. Unyan, and Mr. Clavering then rose to meet his visitor.

'How do you do, Mr. Unyan?' he asked. 'You have arrived at Arbela this evening, I suppose?'

'Yes, sir,' replied Hugh, 'somewhere about three hours ago, and was happy to find all well there and Kathleen quite ready for to-morrow.'

'I am glad of that. At what time does the wedding take place?' asked Mr. Clavering.

'At ten o'clock, I believe,' was the answer. 'It is to be a very quiet affair, you know; I suppose Kathleen has some feeling of respect for the memory of her father.'

'I suppose she has,' said Mr. Clavering dryly. 'Is her ladyship well?'

'Quite, thank you; of course she is a little upset, and naturally enough too, at the thoughts of losing Kathleen,' said Hugh, who did not exactly appreciate Mr. Clavering's manner.

It was gentlemanly and exceedingly polite, but there was a tone of distance in it, a reminder that they were not talking as equals. It was nature with the master of Clonmore, who, as has been said, had a horror of all affectation. At the same time Hugh's manners contrasted favourably with his sister's ; though he was not so real as he used to be, yet he was far from being pretentious even now.

'She is likely to be upset, she was so *very* fond of Kathleen,' said Mr. Clavering, mentally reflecting that her ladyship never had been, nor ever would be, '*very* fond' of anyone except herself.

'You wished to see me on business, did you not ?' asked Hugh, anxious to bring such a forced conversation to an end, and to put himself in possession of five thousand pounds.

'Yes, I did,' answered the master of Clonmore, his manner changing now that he was coming to a matter with Hugh which was business, and also a fulfilling of one of Sir Patrick's last requests. 'As I mentioned in my letter to you, Sir Patrick, by a codicil to his will, of which I am the sole executor, left five thousand pounds to you, to be given on the eve of your marriage with Miss O'Moore. Strange to say, this money is not invested, it is all in notes, and I have to hand them to you. They are the very same notes which Sir Patrick gave me, and I must beg of you a receipt for the money.'

'Certainly, Mr. Clavering,' said Hugh with a smile; 'that is very little to do for so handsome a sum.'

'The notes are in this room, in one of these drawers,' said Mr. Clavering, as he took his keys from his pocket and proceeded to unlock a drawer in his writing-table.

'I hope that I shan't get robbed on my way home; I might, you know,' remarked Hugh carelessly, as he looked towards the unshuttered windows of the library, 'if anyone saw me through one of those windows.'

'No fear of that, Mr. Unyan,' replied Mr. Clavering, who, nevertheless, gave a glance towards the lawn as he recalled Mike O'Leary's attempt upon his life.

'Hullo!' said Hugh, 'I'm sure that I saw a face pressed against that pane of glass, and he walked over to the library window.

'Only imagination, Mr. Unyan, I should think,' replied Mr. Clavering.

But the blind boy started, and suggested audibly, 'O'Crotty.'

'No, no, Pat; don't you be alarmed,' said Mr. Clavering assuringly, as he counted the notes for Hugh. 'Why your father forgave me before he died, my boy! You told me so.'

'Yes, maybe; but faith, I wouldn't give much for O'Crotty's word,' said the blind boy.

Meanwhile Hugh, in order to satisfy himself, had thrown open one of the windows and peered out into the darkness; but as he saw no one there, he supposed it was imagination, though certainly a very strong one; so he shut the window and returned to the writing-table.

'No one there, I suppose,' said Mr. Clavering, as he prepared a paper for Hugh to sign.

'No, no one, sir; it must have been fancy; but I could almost swear that I did see someone,' replied Hugh.

'It was very likely the shadow of a tree or something of that sort,' remarked Mr. Clavering carelessly. 'Just sign this paper, Mr. Unyan, please; and here are the notes—they are quite correct.'

Hugh signed as he was told to do, and received the notes, which he placed in his breast-pocket.

Mr. Clavering did not forget the duties of hospitality, so he rang the bell and ordered wine.

'I wish to have the pleasure, Mr. Unyan,' he said, as he poured out some wine, 'of drinking your health, and Miss O'Moore's, in my own house, and with you. Here is to your very good health, and to Miss O'Moore's happiness. I drink for my son as well as for my-self.'

'I thank you for your kindness, sir,' replied Hugh; 'I trust that I may in every way prove myself worthy of Kathleen.'

Pat O'Leary had been very uncomfortable since the sight of the supposed face at the window; he fidgeted in his chair, and seemed altogether so ill at ease that Mr. Clavering asked him how it was that he appeared so alarmed.

'Shure, yer 'oner, I'm fearin' for you. Has the gintleman seen anyone again?' asked Pat.

'No, my boy,' replied Hugh cheerily; 'I only thought I saw somebody. Don't you mind; it was very foolish of me to make any remark.'

Scarcely had Hugh finished his sentence

when Mr. Clavering, who was turned towards the window, exclaimed: 'By Jove! there is some one there, and it's that ruffian O'Crotty, too!' He ran to the window, threw it open, and, without hesitation, jumped out on the terrace. Hugh followed quickly, and found Mr. Clavering engaged in a struggle with a man. The blind boy screamed, at the same time running out into the hall and calling, 'Murther, murther!' at the top of his voice.

Meantime Hugh, who in vain tried to join in the struggle, or at any rate held back from doing so, saw that Mr. Clavering's strength was going. At the same moment, O'Crotty, for it was he, freed himself from his antagonist's grasp, discharged a pistol, happily without success, then darted across the lawn, hotly pursued.

He ran like a deer; the servants were now in full pursuit, but he distanced them all except one, whom he felt convinced in his own mind was Mr. Clavering.

This one gained rapidly upon him, for O'Crotty was beginning to lose his wind; the hand was already on his collar, when the ruffian turned round and, with the rapidity of lightning, dealt a deadly blow right at the heart of his pursuer. 'Take that, an' that, an' that, Misther Claverin'!' said O'Crotty ferociously, as he dealt him three more blows with his knife, each in itself severe enough to take away life, and then, with a yell of satisfied revenge and of defiance, he bounded off again into the darkness without casting a look at his victim, for he already heard the voices and hurried breathing of his other pursuers.

One of them came up to the dead body.

'By gorra, he's killed him!' said the man, one of Mr. Clavering's own servants, stooping down and surveying the ghastly spectacle as it lay.

'Who's he killed?' asked another servant, coming up.

'The gintleman—the master himself,' answered the other.

'Faith, Misther Claverin's behind; it isn't he.'

'To be sure not, but it's the master to be, of Arbela, who was to be married to-morrow. Oh! wisha, wisha, for poor Miss Kathleen!' said the servant, sympathetically.

'What is this?' asked Mr. Clavering, running up breathlessly, for since his last fray with O'Crotty he had been far less active than before. 'Have you caught the ruffian?'

The servants said nothing, but drew aside while their master approached with a lantern.

'Great God!' he said, as he saw what had happened, with a terrible earnestness upon his face; 'what a dreadful thing for that poor girl!'

He stooped down and felt in vain for any signs of life; it was quite extinct. It was a harrowing sight even for the most hard-hearted. There lay Hugh Unyan, as handsome a young fellow as you would wish to see; his heart had not been one of honour, his life had not been one of principle, nor had he sprung from a good stock. But that was all over now. His body lay there in the vigour and beauty of young manhood, the bridegroom of the to-morrow which never came to him.

Slowly they bore the body back into the

house.   Mr. Clavering followed it with such feelings as he had never experienced before.   He felt deeply for Kathleen, and not only this, but he lamented with sincere sorrow the untimely and terrible end of his son's supplanter.   Willingly, gladly would he have called the young man back to life, could he have done so, and never for a single moment did the ungenerous thought cross his mind that Kathleen would suffer for her heartless treatment of his son.

The body was carried into the dining-room, and then Mr. Clavering sent down the messenger to Arbela, of whose arrival there we have already read.

It was not long before O'Neil returned to Clonmore with the servant sent for him by Mr. Clavering.

He was soon informed of what had happened, and it is needless to say how horrified he was. He related to the master of Clonmore what had already taken place at Arbela, and of how he had unmasked Hugh to Miss O'Moore.

The relation of all this had a visible effect upon Mr. Clavering, who shook O'Neil warmly by the hand, and said :

'You have played the part of a thorough gentleman; you did not consider yourself in the matter, and I am proud, sir, to be able to shake hands with a man who has acted as fearlessly as you have done. I cannot speak evil of the dead in his very presence, but I must say that it was an act of which any man ought to have been ashamed, to deceive Miss O'Moore in the manner in which he did.'

O'Neil told Mr. Clavering his whole history, of how he had reformed, of how he had faithfully promised to prevent

Kathleen's marrying Hugh, or at any rate, without knowing the real character of the man she had chosen to be her husband. He dwelt upon Mrs. Green's story, and of her relationship to Hugh, and therefore to his sister Lady O'Moore, and he told all with such honesty, and proved himself to be a man of such high principle *now*, even if he had not always been so, that Mr Clavering almost forgot the events of the evening in considering the complete re-formation of a gambler, and in admiration of the motives of O'Neil in letting Kathleen know the gaming propensities of Hugh, which he himself had denied on his word of honour as a gentleman.

While Mr. Clavering was listening to O'Neil, a servant, who had been laying-out poor Hugh's body, handed his master the watch and the ring of the unfortunate young man, and also the five thousand pounds in notes which had so recently come into the poor fellow's possession.

'There is a question now, Mr. O'Neil,' said Mr. Clavering, 'which requires consideration. It is with reference to these five thousand pounds.'

'Whom do they belong to?' asked O'Neil, though his thoughts were dwelling upon his dead friend, and the terrible task of breaking the news to Kathleen.

'It is a question of law,' replied Mr. Clavering, 'and it resolves itself into this. Had Mr. Unyan *not* received the notes, they would have gone to the estate and become part of the property of Miss O'Moore; but as it is, they have passed into Mr. Unyan's possession, and by his decease are now the property of his next of kin. Therefore, these five thousand pounds have to be divided among Lady O'Moore, Mrs. Green's father, and their other sister of whom you have spoken.'

'Then can poor Mrs. Green get none of it?' asked O'Neil anxiously, on behalf of his real reformer.

'No, I fear not,' replied Mr. Clavering, 'unless Lady O'Moore resigns her claim in favour of a poorer relative.'

'Do you think she will do so?'

'I am sure that she will not,' was the only answer Mr. Clavering vouchsafed.

The two gentlemen did not go to bed that night; their brains were too active for sleep, and their minds too distraught. O'Neil's was in a worse state than Mr. Clavering's; he had undergone a great deal at Arbela, and more since he came to Clonmore.

They talked upon various subjects

connected with Kathleen and poor Hugh throughout the night. Arrangements were made with reference to the coroner's inquest, and suggestions as to the best way of breaking the terrible news to Kathleen and to Lady O'Moore.

'As to her ladyship,' said Mr. Clavering, 'you need not study nicety of expression, nor the manner in which you will break the news to her. She is, between ourselves, the most heartless woman that I ever met. I can assure you that the way in which she took Sir Patrick's death was extraordinary. She is, indeed, a wonderful woman, but wonderful only in want of heart and in scheming cleverness. She probably inherited the latter quality from the Unyan side of her house. You may call my opinion severe, but it is only too true.'

Early the next morning Mr. Clavering accompanied O'Neil to Arbela. On their arrival there they found that Kathleen had been so very ill in the night that the doctor had been sent for. She was now in a high state of fever and perfectly unconscious, so that for the time being they were relieved from breaking the evil tidings to her.

Mr. Clavering deputed himself to the task of telling Lady O'Moore what had happened to her unfortunate brother. She *really* was surprised, nay, shocked at the terrible news, and evinced more womanly feeling than he had thought her capable of.

During the next week all the melancholy details attending upon Hugh's death were carried out. Kathleen continued dangerously ill and utterly unconscious of what was going on.

At last her life was despaired of, and

Mr. Clavering, upon his own responsibility, sent to Dublin and engaged the continuous services of a clever physician.

Lady O'Moore was unequal to the occasion, and so was her housekeeper. Mr. O'Neil suggested Mrs. Green as a nurse for Kathleen, without even mentioning the suggestion to her ladyship; Mr. Clavering was willing to accept it, and so the widow was sent for post-haste. At the same time, when poor Hugh's funeral was over, Lady O'Moore declared her intention of going to Dublin immediately. She could not, she said, stay any longer in Inchigeela; it had been to her a place of continual sorrow, the end of it being Hugh's death. She did not state that she meant to get married again. Mr. Clavering was delighted to see her leave Arbela; he took a real interest in Kathleen's welfare, but as to her ladyship, he did not care how soon she took her departure nor how long she stayed away.

The morning after Lady O'Moore left Arbela, Mrs. Green arrived; the doctor was already there. The poor widow had, according to O'Neil's directions, left her little one in charge of his wife in Dublin, so she arrived alone, glad at heart thus to have an opportunity of befriending Kathleen.

The days passed away, and there were but few signs of improvement in the patient; Mrs. Green was unremitting in her attentions, until at length Kathleen was pronounced free from fever; but it was added that her weakness was extreme, and that though she was in a measure convalescent, yet all danger of a relapse was not over.

Mr. O'Neil returned to Dublin, and Mr. Clavering from time to time sent him word as to the state of Kathleen's health.

It is needless to say that the terrible circumstances of Hugh's death caused a feeling of intense sympathy, not only among the cottagers of Inchigeela, but also among the gentry who lived round; but it was mostly for Kathleen's sake, for her stepmother was not a favourite, while poor Hugh was almost unknown.

It is curious that though search was made in every direction for O'Crotty, and the best organisation of pursuit established, up to three weeks after Hugh's death no traces of the savage murderer could be discovered.

CHAPTER II.

COMING BACK TO LIFE AND TO SORROW.

' He tempers the wind to the shorn lamb.'
' The ravell'd sleeve of care.'

FIVE weeks after the sad events recorded
in the last two chapters, poor Kathleen
showed signs of returning to life. In her
body there was the dreary ending of well-
nigh spent pain, but her mind was only
beginning to realise the fact that something dreadful had happened to her. She
could not definitely recall what O'Neil had
told her about Hugh ; it was something bad ·

of him, that she remembered, but she was curiously anxious to recollect what it was. Her mind was restless upon the subject, and she did not know how to satisfy it, or, in her waking from sickness, to whom she should apply for information. She had an idea that throughout her illness there had been some one watching by her bedside whom she had once known, but she was unable to put in their proper place the features of her nurse, or to recall under what circumstances in her life she had before seen them.

'Snatched from the jaws of death' is a common expression, and yet it applied exactly to Kathleen's state during her illness. Not only was she near to death, but she actually was dead to life. It was a great mercy that she had been so, without any cravings to know her real position with reference to Hugh, or to take interest in what was going on. It was indeed a tempering of wind to sorrow, and she could now better bear her trouble than she could have done had the blast blown suddenly upon her. She felt that something grievous had fallen upon her; she was prepared to hear what it was, or rather, more than that, she longed to do so.

It has been said that the time of convalescence after a severe illness is a time of quiet pleasure. This is probable in some cases where the invalid is welcomed back to life with the joy and gratitude of warm hearts that have been almost broken with anxieties on his account. And besides this, the invalid's own feelings have much to do with such a state of pleasure; there may be freedom from intense pain and a delight at being able to return to an existence which for him is happy and free from care. But how is it with the sick man or woman who, like Kathleen, has come back to new sorrow and new mental pain? Illness has been to them a sleep of the mind; it *has* 'knit up the ravell'd sleeve of care,' and the awakening from that bed of sickness and from that mental somnolence is the beginning of a life to them the sorrows of which swallow up in oblivion the pains of the sick-bed so recently quitted.

There are recoveries from illness which are full of grief instead of quiet pleasure.

Take for example the case of a mother ill at the same time with her child. The child dies; the mother, in the extremity of her illness, knows nothing of this; but when she recovers, the first conscious question

framed by her lips is, 'Where is my child?'
And the answer begins for her a new life
of sorrow.

Or the case of another, such as Kathleen's, where a sudden shock is the cause
of an illness accompanied by unconscious-
ness. Scarcely is the shock sooner felt
than it is forgotten. But if the patient
recovers, then the cause of the sickness is
remembered, indistinctly perhaps at first,
and tempered by time and circumstances,
but yet sufficient to make life, for the time
at any rate, a burden and a care. With
such as these, who have not tasted of
death during their sickness, to them new
life is sometimes living death.

What must have been the feelings of
those who did taste of death, who really
did cross the dark flood, and yet were
recalled by the voice of One who is Lord

of the dead and of the living ? How much
of the bitterness of death did they taste,
and how much of the sweetness that lay
beyond it ? We cannot fathom the
mystery of that intermediate state, we
cannot say whether it is or is not a living
though unconscious sleep.

One morning Kathleen drew aside the
curtain of her bed and saw Mrs. Green
seated at a table. Then she remembered
under what circumstances she had seen the
gambler's wife, how she had heard from
her, how she herself had answered that
letter ; and finally, at first like an indistinct
dream, but afterwards as a clear fact, she
recalled her interview with O'Neil in the
drawing-room and the subject of their conversation, and how, to prove his accusation,
he had shown her the promissory note in
Hugh's own handwriting.

'Mrs. Green,' she said faintly, 'what time is it?'

'Well, bless me, if that ain't the first word you've spoke, Miss Kathleen! It's five o'clock, and I'm just going to light a lamp.'

'And when was the wedding to have taken place?' asked Kathleen, who had no idea of the length of time she had been ill. 'I mean, you know, if I hadn't been ill.'

'Five weeks ago yesterday,' answered Mrs. Green, stirring the fire.

She was a wary nurse, and she had made up her mind to leave the news of Hugh's death, or of anything that might arouse Kathleen's suspicions, to Mr. Clavering's telling; she was afraid lest she might sadly bungle matters.

'Five weeks ago!' exclaimed Kathleen.

'Is it possible? And where are Mr.
Unyan and mamma? Let me see one of
them.'

'You can't see either of them, Miss
Kathleen: 'your ma's in Dublin, and Mr.
Unyan ain't 'ere nohows!'

'Mamma in Dublin!' exclaimed Kathleen, again in surprise. 'Why is she there?
why has she left me?'

'She was so terribly upset, miss, by the
awful news——'

Mrs. Green had nearly put her foot into
it this time, but she pulled up just in
time.

'By the awful news of what?' asked
Kathleen, during which question the
widow framed an answer.

'News of your illness, Miss Kathleen.
She seems much attached to you!' hazarded
Mrs. Green, by way of comfort.

'Then it is something quite new; if she had really cared for me, she would not have left me alone,' answered Kathleen, with the pettishness of an invalid. 'And Mr. Unyan, where is he?' she asked, hoping for a more satisfactory answer from Mrs. Green.

'I don't know, miss,' replied the widow gravely, turning her back upon the sick-bed lest its occupant might see something in her face which would betray the terrible truth. 'He left 'ere some time back, an' I've never set eyes on him since.'

'Did he never come to ask for me, nor send a message for me?' asked Kathleen, whose mind was revolving the apparently strange conduct of her lover.

'No, miss; Mr. O'Neil sent for me to come an' nurse you, an' when I came, Mr. Unyan was gone.'

' I expect, then,' said Kathleen, putting two and two together according to her best light, ' that Mr. O'Neil told him all about it and that then Hugh ran away. Poor fellow, I never could have married him!'

Mrs. Green took no notice of what her patient was saying. She fancied that Kathleen was once more wandering unconsciously, until a faint voice called her by name and a slender hand beckoned her to the bedside.

' Kneel on the floor, Mrs. Green, by my bed; I have something to ask and something to say. Where is Mr. Clavering ?'

' Lor', miss, you can see 'im to-morrow mornin', 'e's never left this 'ouse since yer ma went away; 'e's watched you tenderly, an' it's my opinion wi' them quiet ways 'e 'as, that Mr. Claverin' ought to be a woman,' this being intended for a compliment by the poor widow.

'Then I may see him to-morrow morning?' said Kathleen questioningly.

'Yes, to be sure, miss; but no more questions to-night. Mr. Claverin' will tell you everythink to-morrow far better nor I can.'

'I do not want to ask any more questions,' said Kathleen quietly, 'but I want to ask your forgiveness, poor Mrs. Green. You were right and I was wrong; Hugh is a gambler, and when I was satisfied of it, then it almost broke my heart. Oh! it did indeed, not only because I could not marry him, but because he whom I loved far, far better than anyone or anything in this world had lied to me whom he professed to love well enough to ask to become his wife. That is what made me ill; it made me worse than if I had seen him lying dead at my feet.'

Mrs. Green felt almost tempted to break the news of Hugh's death to Kathleen **at** this favourable opportunity; but she did not yield to the temptation, fearing, as she did, the effects such a disclosure might have on her patient, who was sobbing now at the recollection of Hugh's dishonour in her eyes.

'Lor', miss, don't take on so; it was all for the best,' said Mrs. Green, with the sympathy of her class, although the sentiment came from her warm heart.

'You will forgive me for the wrong I have done you, will you not?' asked Kathleen. 'I could not believe your word against his, because I loved him so; and in my love for him there was no wish to deceive him or to conceal anything from him.   I only dreaded lest I was not open enough ; and I thought that his love was the same, but it was not.   No, I was un- willing to admit that he was in the wrong even when the truth came to light.   You will forgive me, Mrs. Green ?'

' In course, miss ; not as 'ow there is any- thing to forgive.   Love is blind, so they says ; an' yours wouldn't see, I s'pose it was that,' said the poor woman, who went a good deal by ' sayings.'

Shortly after this, Kathleen dropped asleep.   She passed a very quiet night and felt better on the following morning, although the grief still gnawed at her heart and made her convalescence painful. She asked to see Mr. Clavering, and he came in a few minutes ; he kissed her gently upon the forehead and asked how she was, as the sympathetic tears rose to his eyes. Was she not an orphan; was she not deprived of the man she loved best; was she not the dearest being on earth to his only son?

Mrs. Green left the room, and then Mr. Clavering, by skilful preparation, led the way towards telling Kathleen the dreadful circumstances of Hugh's death. And when he had told her all and was expressing his kindly sympathy, there was no answer, only a frequent sobbing, caused by the anguish of an almost broken heart. He pressed her little worn hand in his own, and then he left her. Never again did Kathleen refer to Hugh's death, never did a single word of it cross her lips; it was a subject buried from the world deep in the recesses of her own heart, and she pondered over it and nursed it as her own peculiar grief.

Nor did Mr. Clavering touch upon the sad event again, and he resolved not to do so until Kathleen herself began the subject. He cautioned Mrs. Green upon the point, and she, too, was mute.

Little by little did Kathleen's strength come back, and she was enabled to spend her Christmas-day before her bedroom fire, propped up with pillows which were arranged by Mr. Clavering's own hands.

But it was in vain that he tried to bring a smile to Kathleen's lips; her thoughts seemed ever centred upon one subject, and vacant upon everything else but that.

Little Pat O'Leary, who was growing out of knowledge, had also taken up his abode at Arbela. He would not have done so, nor for that matter would Mr. Clavering, if her ladyship had been there. Lady O'Moore was virtually mistress of

Arbela, but Mr. Clavering had his own ideas upon that subject; he imagined that she would marry again, although by so doing she would lose half her income and her house. But then he knew her thoroughly; a woman who from nothing had raised herself to the dignity of a baronet's wife, would probably, on becoming a baronet's widow, endeavour to advance a step or two higher on the social ladder, or might even go up three or four steps at a time.

Thus he had no misgivings as to his residing at Arbela; he was there for Sir Patrick's sake, to look after the interests of his friend's only child, who, if she was not already mistress of the house, would soon be so. Mr. Clavering expected daily to have news from Dublin to say that her ladyship was about to enter upon another

state of wedlock.   True, that her husband
was not yet dead a year, nor her brother
three months; but then she was Lady
O'Moore, and when Mr. Clavering recol-
lected this, he knew that all sense of
decency would be laid aside if it stood in
the way of her own pleasure or of her
advantage.   He had already sent her the
third part of Hugh's five thousand pounds,
with a polite note intimating that the rest
had been duly divided and forwarded to
her brother and sister in New York, of
whose status there she was doubtless
aware.

Mr. Clavering found his task of trying
to raise Kathleen's spirits not only difficult
but useless.   Pat's music was sometimes
called into requisition; but as Kathleen
would never let him play any but the
saddest strains, the result was generally a

fit of weeping, or if not that, it was easy to see by her quivering lip and the expression of pain which crossed her countenance, that her thoughts were dwelling even more forcibly upon the past. Then the master of Clonmore made the music cease, and would read to her; but his audience showed so little interest that in his despair he appealed to the doctors for advice, which resulted in the move spoken of in a later chapter.

CHAPTER III.

A COUNTESS IN WHOM WAS NO GUILE.

' O most delicate fiend !'
' Who is't can read a woman ?'

LADY O'MOORE, preparatory to leaving for
Dublin, had engaged a furnished house
there, in Merrion Street. It was an old
house, not far from the very fine mansion
then occupied by Colonel Conyngham's
family, but was spacious; and its furniture,
though tarnished, lent an antiquity to the
place which satisfied her ladyship, who
had a now established horror of 'anything
new' in the way of house decoration; this

horror was *comme il faut,* and that is the reason why she felt it.

She attired herself in very good taste, and the heavy mourning suited her. No 'widow's sombre cap concealed her once luxuriant hair,' because her locks were still abundant, and were without a single thread of that silver which tells of the advance of years, or the premature old age which is the accompaniment of deep sorrow.

Lady O'Moore, who had before held her sway as Sir Patrick's wife, now held it as his widow, not with the brilliant receptions of old, but in a quiet manner and suitable to so short a period after so heavy a bereavement. Many of her old friends called upon her; Lady O'Moore was still a person worth knowing. Rumours were abroad concerning her fabulous jointure; many believed that she had her thousands a year, and when this was doubted by the less credulous, then the more credulous said, 'Look how wealthy Sir Patrick was! Look at her ladyship's carriage, and house, and diamonds, and silks!'

'True,' replied the former, 'but you must remember that Sir Patrick may have left the bulk of his fortune to his daughter. You will see that if Lady O'Moore marries again she loses half her property.' But the people who talked thus were in the minority, and old young men who sighed about the widow's drawing-room, or brought her bouquets of flowers, pooh-poohed the idea, and said that a generous man like Sir Patrick, who had likewise been the most affectionate of husbands, could not fail to have left his widow amply provided for, whatever she might choose to do.

What wonder was it, they asked, if Lady O'Moore did marry again? She was still young, still fair, and had many suitors. The only question worth considering was this: Whom should she marry?

This was indeed a question. Her ladyship coquetted with many, she let them dance attendance on her, asked them to dinner—when there were other ladies present; in fact she began seriously to think of engaging a chaperon for herself. She was so young, so admired, so innocent and guileless, that we could scarcely wonder had she done so, could we?

But November and December and January and part of February passed away, and her ladyship was still a widow, and her heart continued cold as the weather. Still a widow! Why her husband had only been dead just a year! No matter, he was almost forgotten, and her mourning for him did not go as deep as her crape. And there was her brother's death? Surely she had been a little fond of him! Yes, perhaps so. And was she not anxious about her step-daughter's health? Oh yes; she had written three or four times to Mr. Clavering to make inquiries after her, and in one of his letters she had been reminded of her brother's and sister's status in New York, and had received her exact third share of Hugh's five thousand pounds—sixteen hundred and sixty pounds thirteen shillings and fourpence. Yes, the pounds were very well, very well indeed; but the thirteen shillings and fourpence, as sent to her by Mr. Clavering, were so very trying to her nerves, because they brought her down to the level of her brother and sister in New York. To them, the thirteen and fourpence might alone have proved acceptable; but to her, Lady O'Moore! well, they had their value: they were two lawyer's fees.

There was someone of whom her ladyship thought more than she had ever thought of Sir Patrick, someone whom she loved far better than she had ever loved Hugh, someone for whom she felt more anxious than she had ever felt for Kathleen; and who was this—a new lover? No, herself. This was the secret of her heartlessness, the reason of her schemings: I love myself because I know myself loves me.

It was once asked, what reward was there in a man's loving another who loved him in turn? There was no merit certainly in Lady O'Moore loving herself, and the reward she should have for her selfishness was yet to come. It was not what she expected; she hoped always to be gratified : but it was a vain hope for her or for anyone to entertain in this chequered life of light and shadow.

At length there came to her ladyship's bower an exceeding young old man, and he was destined to be the successful suitor. Was he amiable, or good-looking? Neither; but he had a title, and was reported to be rich.

Monsieur le Comte Naufrancs de Fleurigny was a French refugee. Of noble birth, as his title indicates, he had lived upon his estate, so he stated, until the beginning of the troubles raised in France, when he fled to England.

He had not returned to his country, as some nobler refugees than he had done, when summoned by their emperor ; but had further retreated from London to Dublin.

Monsieur le Comte was an exquisite dandy and bore his age well. He possessed a title, but he was not wealthy, although he had an inordinate love for play. He made stealthy and polite advances towards Lady O'Moore, dwelt with becoming modesty upon his own fortune, did not seek to pry into her ladyship's, since he saw so many substantial proofs of wealth around her and heard so much of it, until he at length resolved to put his 'ange,' as he called her, to the test, and begged of her to become his loving countess.

Lady O'Moore took a day or two for consideration, was just a little coy, a little hesitating, but she consented with gladness to his request. A countess! Lucy Unyan,

Lady O'Moore, Comtesse Naufrancs de Fleurigny; she had almost reached the pinnacle of fame! She soon lessened her mourning, had her paper and envelopes stamped with an earl's coronet, and before the end of March was married to the count.

Then she wrote to Mr. Clavering on some of her new paper, thinking that it, at any rate, would impress him with a sense of her greatness.

But it did nothing of the kind. She informed him of her marriage, that she was aware how she had lessened her income, and deprived herself of Arbela: but she had done so rather than act against her own conscience, and against the 'pure love of a man who had married *her for her own sake,* and not for the sake of money or estate.' But this was not all. The tone of the letter was lofty until its final paragraph : in that she assumed the tone of one who deserved but little, but who dared to trust to the generosity of her stepdaughter for a marriage portion.

Mr. Clavering received the letter with a smile of contempt ; he gave it to Kathleen to read, and concluded for himself that she would not consider herself bound to make a pecuniary present to one who had shown heartlessness and most indecent haste in marrying again.

He was, however, wrong in his conclusion, for the last paragraph of the letter received the attention of Kathleen, and drew from her the following remarks.

'You think, Mr. Clavering, I know, that my stepmother's request is monstrous,' she said.

'I do,' was Mr. Clavering's answer.

'She has already received her share of five thousand pounds and has five hundred a year to live on, which to my mind is far more than such a person deserves. They say that her husband has money, let him support her! My advice to you, Kathleen, is this: do not give her another penny beyond what she is entitled to by your father's will, and refuse to have any further communications with her.'

'I shall follow your advice, Mr. Claver-ing, to a certain extent; I will have no further communications with her after to-day, but I desire you to forward her five thousand pounds, intimating to her my determination to have no more to do with her,' said Kathleen, who was resolved to carry this through.

'I cannot see the reason for this weak generosity of yours, Kathleen,' said Mr:

Clavering, discontentedly; 'Lady O'Moore, or rather the Countess Naufrancs, does not deserve it, and such a sum seems to me like a tacit approval on your part of her conduct.'

'Not at all,' replied Kathleen; 'I leave it to you to word the letter which contains a draft for five thousand pounds, and you must be careful to fix no impression of that sort upon her mind. My reasons for my conduct are these, and I think you will approve of them.

'My poor father on his death-bed said to me, I remember as well as though I heard it all yesterday, in spite of what has happened; "Should she *not* marry again," he said, "be kind to her, child; treat her with respect—"' here Kathleen hesitated a moment, and a curious look of woe came into her face. She remembered that Sir

Patrick's next words had been, 'treat her with respect, not as your husband's sister, but as your own father's wife.' Then she continued, ' " treat her with respect, as your own father's wife." '

'You would have done so, Kathleen,' said Mr. Clavering, 'had she continued faithful to your father's memory, or had she in any way proved herself worthy of respect, but as it is I cannot see that you are called upon to make the sacrifice you contemplate. You have a generous heart, but this is a matter which places itself beyond my pity but deep in my contempt.'

'My father told me to be kind to her,' continued Kathleen, in a tone which showed her resolve to carry her point, 'and I should be the most ungrateful of daughters did I not carry out his request. In doing that alone, I should be erecting ·

a monument to his memory as a proof of my love, and surely in going a little beyond it I am carrying out in a more worthy manner his sincere wish, that his widow should receive from his only child kindness and consideration. When you write to the countess, tell her, that in accordance with my father's last wish, I have pleasure in sending her the sum of five thousand pounds, but that my heart bleeds to think of how soon she has forgotten him, who, in his love for her, gratified her every whim without even a murmur.'

'I will do so, Kathleen,' replied Mr. Clavering; 'your motives are noble, and I will say no more against your sending the money; but as the executor of your father's will, as his best friend, and in the interest I take in you, not only for your own sake, but because you were left to my

care by him, should you require it, I shall
state very clearly to the countess that any
further demands for money, in fact any
further letters on whatsoever subject, will
never be answered.'

Mr. Clavering wrote the following letter
to the Countess Naufrancs. After giving
her her full title at the top of the page, he
began :

'Madame,

'At Miss O'Moore's request, I
forward you a draft for five thousand
pounds; permit me to add that I have
very great repugnance in doing so.

'But Miss O'Moore, desiring to carry
out the expressed wish of her late father,
that she should be kind to you, and show
you all due respect (in the event of your
not marrying again), has gone even further,

and in her generosity has made you the enclosed handsome present.

'However, she wishes me to add that your heartless and indecent conduct has caused her much surprise and much pain; or rather, to sum up the expression, she is, naturally, very much disgusted.

'It is indeed a wonder that so devoted a husband as Sir Patrick was to you should be so soon forgotten, and that his place in your heart should be so soon filled by another, who may be rich, who has a title, but who is, from trustworthy accounts, a man of very doubtful character.

'I am requested to state that any further demand you may make for money will receive no attention, nor will any letter of yours, on any subject, be answered. Miss O'Moore, having more than fulfilled her duty, is rightly anxious to break off all connection with one who has proved herself to be such as yourself.

　　　‘I am, madame,

　　　　　‘Your obedient servant,

　　　　　　　‘CECIL CLAVERING.’

This was received by the countess, and though she was surprised at Kathleen’s present and delighted with it, yet Mr. Clavering’s letter was a bitter pill for her to swallow; but she pocketed her choler and the draft.

The life of a countess is not without care, however easily the title may have come to her, or however ancient may be its origin.

It has its disappointments, too, and the Countess Naufrancs soon learnt this. About a month after her marriage, the count, with many endearing terms, got his

wife to speak of her property. She told
him that she now had but five hundred a
year, that her estate by her second marriage had passed into the hands of her
daughter, and then, when she saw his
wrath rising, she tried to appease it by a
mention of the five thousand pounds.

But it was in vain; the Frenchman was
furious, he swore that he would take her
life, that he would starve her; he turned
off the servants, locked her in her own
room, in spite of tears and entreaties to the
contrary.

Née Lucy Unyan had met more than
her match; her husband had a worse
temper than she, he had a stronger will, he
was more cunning, and, if possible, more
heartless. The time of retribution had come,
and during the day he kept her locked in
her room, she recalled Sir Patrick and her

dead child, and repented the step she had taken, all for the sake of a trumpery title.

And when the count calmed down a little, he came and freed her from her imprisonment, but demanded with threats her five thousand pounds. Then she refused ; he threw her upon a sofa and nearly strangled her, until she cried for mercy and gave him up the money.

She would free herself from this wretch, she said ; she could not endure such a life. But then pride thrust itself in the way and drew her an unpleasant picture of herself separated from her husband in some lonely place, no one to speak to and no one to admire her ; but, more than this, there would be her step-daughter to scoff at her, and Mr. Clavering as well, while the world would point its finger of derision at the would-be countess.

In spite of the count's cruelty, in spite of his frequent demands for money and the fact that debts were fast accumulating, she yet was queen of a little circle in Dublin, had her receptions and dinners, and endeavoured to smile before the world, while she wept bitterly when its back was turned upon her. She thought it would be preferable to endure domestic unhappiness to giving up the position she held. She would some day soon find that it was not so.

Ah! Madame la Comtesse Naufrancs de Fleurigny, your face tells a different tale to what it once told ; love has never found its way to your heart, grief has never yet learnt how to silver your hair, but something is making an impression upon you. Are you growing older ? is that the reason ? No, but you are beginning to learn what

trouble is under the tyranny of a cruel and
unprincipled master ; a smiling face to the
world, and eyes red with weeping when
you are alone with him, are more than you
can well carry off. At last you find it
difficult to act two parts ; the tears come
readily enough, but the smile is forced, and
in a spirit of sorrow that the past is past,
rather than in a spirit of repentance, you
are losing your good looks and your happi-
piness, because a man has found your
dearest idol to be *self*, and is by degrees
knocking it to pieces.

CHAPTER IV.

TORRES VEDRAS AND FUENTES DE ONORO.

' 'Tis an ill wind that blows nobody good.'

WELLINGTON had his whole army safely disposed behind the impregnable lines of Torres Vedras, in the month of October, 1810. He took up his station in the front, and his head-quarters were at Pero Negro, near the Secorra, a rock from which a system of telegraphs was established with the whole line.

Massena in vain tried to find a spot where he might break through. There was a skirmish at Sobral on the 14th of

October, in which the 71st regiment distinguished itself.

The French army had great difficulty
in procuring provisions, and effected a
miserable maintenance for itself.   Portugal
and Spain sought revenge for desolate
homes and slaughtered kinsfolk, while the
British had a free communication with
their fleet and the sea, and had an
abundance of provisions.   The forts were
garrisoned by native troops; the duty
was light, and officers and men enjoyed
rural life in a beautiful and romantic
country.

Throughout the month of October
Frank's spirits were at their ebb.   His
brother officers were beginning to enjoy
fox-hunting, while he, though he occa-
sionally joined the field, yet joined it
as something to be done, and did not

take part in it with that zest which be-
longed to his old days of going across
country.

Murphy, on the other hand, was delighted at this introduction of home life
into the campaign. He did his best to
encourage his master on to sport ; he used
to say, ' Plaise, go to hounds to-day, yer
'oner, an' forgit Miss Kathleen for once
in a way, if it's only for the pleasure
of me gettin' ye ready an' cleanin' yer
boots.'

At length the news of Hugh's death
reached Frank. To say that he regretted
the occurrence would be untrue and contrary to nature. He was sorry for Kathleen's sake, as he wrote to his father, but
to himself it opened up a new world, or
rather revived the old days, and bade him
hope again. Yes, it was wonderful to see

how his spirits came back to him. His hope had been deferred, it had been crushed, but now once more it was bidden to arise and to live, until it might be realised.

It was with a different heart and in a different frame of mind that Frank got ready for the first run when he had answered his father's letter which brought to him the tidings of Hugh's death. His friends noticed the change in him for the better, but to none of them was it so apparent as it was to his faithful servant, Murphy.

'Faith, yer 'oner, it's a mighty change has came over ye, all of a sudden, and the blight seems to have entirely left the potatoes,' he said while he was assisting his master to make a shift for a hunting turn-out.

'I feel much better, Murphy,' said Frank, cheerily; 'there's a chance, I hear, of my being sént home with despatches some of these days.'

'Faith, sur, I'm thinkin' that that is not entirely the reason of your good spirits,' said Murphy laconically.

'How do you mean, Murphy?' asked his superior officer. 'But come, put down those boots; remember you are a corporal now, and that isn't your work.'

'Faith, yer oner, it's my work if I choose to undertake it, an' I'd rather go back to a private than be obliged to lave off cleanin' your boots. But excusin' the liberty I take, I believe it's all owin' to news of Miss Kathleen which has made you like quicksilver all of a sudden,' remarked Murphy, pausing in the midst of his labours.

'Well, it may be, Murphy,' replied Frank; ' but there is one piece of news which may not please you.'

'An' what's that, yer 'oner ?'

'Why this, that my father is now living in London, and has no intention of residing any more at Clonmore; his life has been attempted three times. So that if I should be sent home with despatches, and you should come with me, you will have to choose between living at Inchigeela near to Widow Machree, or else living with me in London. What choice will you make, Murphy ?'

'Faith, :' ·   ¬ur livin' near the widdy is uncertain work, and I'd rather live in Lunnon wi' yer oner.'

A short time afterwards Frank mounted his horse, saying as he did so: 'Well, I'm in the field once more, and hope to have

a good run, as I'm in the humour for it,'
and then he rode off.

'Faith, thin, an' may the A'mighty give
yer 'oner a good run,' said Murphy, looking after his master ; 'may ye be in at the
death, an' kill her yerself. There never
stepped a braver gintleman than yerself,
an' I'll thank heaven to send me home wi'
you when ye go; an' maybe there's a
better lass waitin' for me in Lunnon or
elsewhere than Widdy Machree, who will
take a greater fancy to a soldier than she
ever did to a gineral servant, for I was
nothing better.'

The weather was ⌐⌐ _ ⌐⌐⌐ 'y fine at
this period, and the face of war put on a
cheerful expression. Too much time was
not wasted in sport, but new works were
constructed, until the British position became absolutely impregnable, and Massena

in despair, withdrew towards the end of October to Santarem.

In January, 1811, Graham achieved a victory over the French. He was assisted by Major Duncan, while the Spaniards were guilty of dastardly treachery. A sanguinary conflict took place which lasted about an hour and a half; the British numbered only eleven hundred men, while the French lost two thousand soldiers, six guns, an eagle, two generals and four hundred men taken prisoners.

On the 2nd of March the French were driven from their position at Pombal by the 95th, and on the 3rd of May the battle of Fuentes de Onoro took place.

This village was occupied by five chosen battalions of the first and third divisions.

General Loison attacked them; he was bravely met and held in check, until their commander, Colonel Williams of the 60th regiment, fell severely wounded. The enemy's efforts were nearly crowned with success, when the 24th, 71st, and 79th came down from · the main position to their assistance, made a spirited charge, and drove the enemy from the village.

On the fourth of the month Massena arrived, and on the fifth a furious attack was made on the British right by some French cavalry under Montbrun. The village of Fuentes de Onoro again became the main object of contention. Drouet was ordered to take it at the moment when the British right wing was turned by Montbrun's cavalry. There was, however, a delay of two hours in the execution of this order. The village was defended by the gallant third division—' the fighting third'—but there was so tremendous a cannonade against them that they began to give way. Then it was that the 88th under Colonel Wallace, led on by Major-General Mackinnon moved up to support them, with the cry of 'Faugh-a-ballagh.' The regiment made a desperate charge through the streets, and drove out the enemy with immense loss.

Frank was well to the front, but came out of the conflict unscathed. He was highly complimented upon his bravery, for his company were foremost in the fight. Murphy was not so fortunate; he lost his left arm in the fray, but fought on until he dropped from loss of blood.

Frank's bravery had its reward, for two months afterwards he was ordered home with despatches, being on the sick list at the time; and Murphy accompanied him, as his fighting days were ended.

For us, then, the campaign in the Peninsula is over, but not for all. There were yet years of weary warfare to come. But at the end of these, British arms were to come out victorious, and the scourge of Europe was to be banished to a lonely isle. How much misery was past, how much misery was to come, and how much of it all was to be attributed to the blood-thirsty ambition of an insatiable tyrant! But thus it must be to the end : 'wars and rumours of wars,' until the beginning of that reign of peace, in which swords shall be turned into ploughshares, and spears into pruning-hooks.

CHAPTER V.

MR. CLAVERING GOES TO LONDON.

'I see men as trees walking.'

THE advice which the doctors gave to Mr. Clavering was this : that change of air and scene was the only thing they could recommend as an aid towards Kathleen's complete recovery. Physically, she was nearly well ; but mentally, far from it. So long, they said, as her grief was nourished by surrounding circumstances, so long it was impossible for her to recover her spirits. Her continued abode at Inchigeela was only bringing the past nearer to her; the house she lived in, the drives she took, all reminded her of Hugh; and not only of his death, which to her was not the greatest sorrow connected with her late lover, but of the deception he had practised towards her.

This it was which galled her; her idea of love, which she had learnt for herself from her own experience, was not only affection, but confidence, and this last complement Hugh had sadly lacked.

Mr. Clavering duly reported the medical advice to Kathleen, and she readily and gladly accepted the idea of change. He fancied that she would raise some objection, but she raised none, simply expressing the opinion that the sooner the change in residence was effected, the better for her.

The month of May came round, and

Mr. Clavering found a trusty steward to take charge of his own estate and another to look after Arbela. Meanwhile he procured a house in London for himself, and Kathleen very willingly consented to share it with him. Then came the question of what should be done with Pat O'Leary; he was given his choice of remaining behind with his mother, and his kith and kin, or of accompanying the master of Clonmore to London. After some deliberation the blind boy decided to accompany his benefactor. Gratitude and affection prompted his decision, but it was hastened by a promise from Mr. Clavering to see if something could not be done in the great city towards restoring the poor child's sight.

The thought of sight was indeed a temptation to Pat; he pictured the world

and its inhabitants as being far more
beautiful than they really are. He did
not realise to what an amount of visible
want and suffering he would be awakened
were his eyes opened for him. But there
was something he looked forward to, even
more than seeing people and things. Mr.
Clavering had talked to him of the glories
of music, of the old masters, and of the
wonderful thoughts they had left upon
paper. He had described to the child
how he might transfer all these beauties
from paper to his own violin, and how he
might render, in the appreciation of his
own soul, echoes of the glorious past into
living notes as worthy recorders of the
transcendent genius which had outlived
its possessors. Sometimes Mr. Clavering
had touched his old 'spinnet' for Pat's
entertainment, and had fingered, perhaps

imperfectly, but certainly with true feeling, passages of beauty which the blind boy transferred to his violin in perfect harmony and correctness of detail. But to read these wonderful compositions for himself was what the boy longed for, and in anticipation of fulfilled desire he almost possessed his sight, when the possible recovery of it was only just talked of.

Mrs. Green, too, must not be forgotten, in the change of residence which was to take place. She had proved herself indispensable to Kathleen, who resolved to take her to London as housekeeper.

Mrs. Machree rather expected this honour, but was pacified by Mr. Clavering, who assured her that he must not leave Clonmore entirely to the possession of strangers. More than this, she was given 'surveillance,' also, over the establishment at Arbela, for Mrs. Rouse—alas for human inconstancy!—who, it will be remembered, had so much objected to the introduction of Lucy Unyan into Sir Patrick's household, had afterwards become Lady O'Moore's friend, and was now housekeeper with the Countess Naufrancs de Fleurigny in Dublin.

At length the preparations for migration were complete; Mr. Clavering, Kathleen, Pat O'Leary, Mrs. Green and child, left Ireland, and were soon installed in a handsome house in the west of London.

It must be recorded here, that detailed directions were given as to Mrs. O'Leary's being taken care of, and that these were fully carried out by the new bailiff at Clonmore and Mrs. Machree, who, some time after Mr. Clavering had left Clonmore, joined their fortunes, and Widow Machree became Mrs. James O'Loghlen. Thus it happened that Murphy's first love mended her heart, if it had ever been injured by his overtures, and found solace in the portly though good-natured person of Mr. Clavering's steward.

As to O'Crotty, he was never found. Perhaps he contented himself with the security of his old hiding-place, or perhaps, after the murder of Hugh, his crowning deed, he feared that 'Ould Ireland' would be too hot for him, and took his departure for America.

O'Neil kept to his promise of never touching another card. He found employment as partner in a thriving business, became a respectable member of society, and had the satisfaction of seeing the colour return to his little wife's cheeks, the smile to her lips, while the tale of care and anxiety left her face.

Thus it behoves us to take leave of some of our friends in Ireland who have had a share, small or important, in our narrative; we shall return thither once more, but meanwhile we must give our attention to England, which now holds those in whom we take, or should take, the greatest interest.

Kathleen's spirits did not return as quickly as Mr. Clavering would have wished to see. He did all in his power to restore them, provided all the diversion he could think of, took care to banish all gloomy topics of conversation, made the house bright and cheerful with guests, but in spite of all, the improvement in Kathleen was not marked.

There was an improvement, but it was only small and gradual.

Mr. Clavering received a letter from his son, during his first few weeks' residence in London, forwarded to him from Clonmore.

Frank expressed great sorrow on Kathleen's account for the calamity which had befallen her in the death of Hugh, and desired his father to express sincere sympathy on his behalf. He went on to say, though of course this was intended for his father's eyes alone, that if Hugh were a gambler, his death was a providential escape from an unhappy marriage for Kathleen. But there was no hint in the letter which could lead anyone to suppose that Frank still looked forward to winning her for himself.

When Mr. Clavering conveyed his son's

sympathy to Kathleen, she only said, ' He is a good fellow, and I trust he may yet find a wife worthy of him.'

' I trust he may,' remarked Mr. Clavering, and then it was for the first time he thought how Frank and Kathleen might yet make one another happy. But as he looked at the pale face, the languid eye, and the lack of interest displayed in all Kathleen's movements, the hope died out of his heart, and he said to himself, ' It is too late now ; she has drunk too deeply of the waters of bitterness ; she is poisoned with them, and there is surely no restorative which can bring her back to her former liveliness, or can even cloud the past and hide it from her memory.'

There was, however, one subject started by Mr. Clavering which seemed to enliven, more than anything else, Kathleen's frame of mind. This was his determination to see some doctor about Pat's blindness. The lids of the child's eyes were not closed by disease; he usually had them shut, but this was from habit, as Mr. Clavering proved, who had his own idea that the boy was suffering from cataract.

It appeared upon inquiry that Pat had not been born blind, but that he was perfectly so before he reached the age of two years.

To support Mr. Clavering's opinion there was this fact: the boy could distinguish bright light from darkness, but only indistinctly, and this led on the master of Clonmore further still to the fact that the disease was a milky cataract of which he had read.

But without waiting or wasting time, Pat was taken to Dr. Young, a then celebrated oculist, who took quite a hopeful view of the case.

The oculist explained to Mr. Clavering the nature of the disease. It was, he said, a milky cataract. He tried several experiments with a bright light, but the difference between this and darkness was scarcely observable to the blind boy. Dr. Young accounted for this by saying that the cataract was bulky, and lay so close to the iris that few or no rays of light could enter between them into the eye; and also that a fluid cataract always assumed a globular form, and consequently had no thin edge through which the rays of light could penetrate. He ended by saying that the removal of the obstacle was mechanical, and appointed a day on which he would perform the operation and remove the sac.

On Mr. Clavering's return home, Kathleen was all anxiety to know what the
surgical opinion was, but she gathered,
without a word, from the radiant expression on the boy's face, that there was
hope.

At length the day for the operation
came round, and Dr. Young, with the
delicate touch of a skilful surgeon, removed
the impediment, and gave his directions as
to further treatment.

Pat was to be kept in a perfectly dark
room for a week; after that, light was to
be gradually let in upon him until he could
bear the full light of day. The oculist
promised to pay the boy one or two visits,
and then received his fee—like many of
the medical and legal professions—as
though money were the last thing to be
thought of, and as though a man could

live without it, and could support life by reading science or by studying law.

Dr. Young's instructions with reference to Pat were carefully carried out. Kathleen took upon herself the duties of attendant, and seemed, for the time being, to be absorbed in another direction than that of her troubles. Little by little Pat's sight came back to him; at first he saw very indistinctly, and could bear but very little light, but after a month's time he went where he listed, wearing a green shade over his eyes. But Mr. Clavering resisted all entreaties made by the boy to be allowed to learn to read and write, and above all to set eyes upon that magic paper on which were set down in mystic characters the glories of music.

Two months passed away, Pat's sight was perfect, and he revelled in his new possession, and gazed upon people and things with awe and wonder. But he was not yet satisfied; he longed to pry into the Sibylline books, and to copy them upon his violin, converting hard black and white into a beautifully illuminated missal, which should have for its colourings the harmony of his strings, and for its gilding the genius of his musical soul.

Then it was that Mr. Clavering could no longer resist the boy's earnest pleadings. Dr. Young gave his consent to his patient's learning to read and write and to his taking music lessons, and masters were engaged for him.

But alas for the alphabet and caligraphy! the boy's appreciation for them was small, while he grasped in a marvellous manner the art of reading music with facility, and more than this, its theory. He delighted in 'counterpoint' and 'fugue,' entered into the study of the imperfect harmony of the 'diminished fifth,' of the harmony of the seventh, of the sensible, of the major mode, and of the dominant major ninth, and so on, until his master gave up his pupil in despair, not because he lacked appreciation or ability, but because the pupil was fit to be the Gamaliel, and because it was the Gamaliel who had to take his place at the feet of his precocious pupil.

Mr. Clavering had long ago expressed an opinion that education would take the soul away from Pat's innate musical genius, but he was wrong. True, the character of his music changed, yet the wild weird melodies of old still lingered in his compositions, but the wild-flower of genius became the garden-flower of cultivation, each of its petals perfect, its perfume and beauty enhanced, and Pat gave promise of being one of the first violinists of the day, while his kind benefactor did all in his power to bring the boy under the notice of leading men in the musical world.

But with his newly-acquired blessing and his undoubted talent Pat continued to be the simple-hearted and affectionate boy of Inchigeela days. His love and gratitude to Mr. Clavering knew no bounds; he had been the boy's best friend from the time he visited the O'Leary cabin until now. He had saved the old violin's existence; he had been wounded for Pat's sake; and finally, he had restored sight to the blind, and had opened a world to the boy, which Pat, in his wildest imaginations, while blind, would have fancied as being, could he have realised it, beyond even the joys of heaven.

CHAPTER VI.

RETURNED HOME WITH DESPATCHES.

'The man that hath no music in himself,
  Nor is not moved with concord of sweet sounds,
  Is fit for treasons.'

FRANK arrived in London about the end of June, and it is needless to say what a welcome he met with from his father. Kathleen, too, expressed her pleasure at seeing him, although the returned warrior was shocked at the difference which had taken place in the appearance and the manner of his former light-hearted school-fellow and companion.

He commented upon this to his father the first evening they sat alone together. They had much to relate to one another— the son, his experiences in Spain ; the father, all that had taken place at Clonmore since Frank's departure. Mr. Clavering entered into the fullest particulars of Hugh's death, explained the way in which the young man's propensities for gambling had come to light, detailed Kathleen's illness and the ineffectual attempts to raise her spirits.

'There is one thing I think you have forgotten to tell me of, father, or rather one person,' said Frank, 'little Pat O'Leary. I haven't seen him this evening.'

'Probably not, Frank,' said Mr. Clavering with a smile ; 'you would never guess what I have done for that dear boy.'

'Well, you have done so much, father, that perhaps you have given him his sight,' replied Frank, little imagining that he had come so near the truth.

'That is the very thing, Frank, or rather I got a surgeon to do it for me; the boy sees perfectly well, and is to-night playing at a concert for the first time. It is only a private one, but still it is a beginning. I cannot tell you what marvellous genius that boy displays for music. It is two months ago now since he first began to study it; he reads it perfectly and has grasped a good deal of the theory of it. As for his other studies, it is of no use trying to induce him to look at them; I am afraid that he will grow up a complete ignoramus in everything but music.'

'There is another person you have not spoken of, father—Lady O'Moore; you told me of her leaving for Dublin at the very beginning of Kathleen's illness. What has become of her ? Is she married again ?'

' You have again come very near the mark, Frank ; her ladyship is now the Countess Naufrancs de Fleurigny, and is leading, I am told, a very unhappy life.'

' I'm delighted to hear it,' said Frank, without hesitation ; ' nothing is bad enough for that woman, in my estimation. From the time she entered Sir Patrick's house until now, she has done nothing but plot and scheme, and has in the end proved herself to be a most heartless woman.'

' She is suffering retribution now, as is generally the case with heartless people who have wounded the feelings of others with as little thought as though they were throwing stones into a pond. It is only when they are themselves injured that they feel and realise the cruelty of their conduct to others. The count is, I hear, a great brute, and although his countess tries to put a good face on to the world, and places her coronet on every available place, yet she has a terrible home life,' said Mr. Clavering, who agreed with his son in thinking that Lady O'Moore deserved her present trouble and more besides.

'And what has become of the Mrs. Green you told me of?' asked Frank.

'She is housekeeper now with us herē, and a very trustworthy and useful one, too. I dare say Murphy will find in her a very agreeable companion,' continued Mr. Clavering, smiling, 'and probably consider her more to his taste and age than Mrs. Machree ever was. He proved himself a faithful servant, did he not?'

'I should think so,' replied Frank ; 'he never seemed happy unless he was serving me in some way or other.   He fought like a lion, but seemed to dislike the Spaniards as much as he did the French.   There are few greater oddities than Murphy in the world, but fewer still with such warm true hearts.'

At this moment the door was opened, and Pat O'Leary entered the room.   What a difference he presented to Frank, who had not seen him for nearly three years! He was now tall and graceful, and his beauty was increased by the expression of his bright eyes.   He looked well in his evening dress, his light hair curled in abundance over his forehead, and in the place of the rough unkempt child of Inchigeela, Frank gazed upon the young gentleman of genius, moulded and cultured

by the hands of his kind father. And
when the boy began to speak, there
was another discernible difference in his
conversation. But 'honour to whom
honour is due,' and Kathleen it was who
had effected this change. During the
incipient stage of the recovery of his sight,
she had given him lessons, and though the
unmistakable brogue was yet there, the
'you' had taken the place of 'ye,' 'with'
of 'wi';' and 'faith, thin,' and expressions
of that kind were as much past and out of
use as were the old clothes of his cabin
days. The boy was a marvel; much was
due to Mr. Clavering for the change, but
there had been good ground to work upon;
the seed had been already there, and the
careful tending and wise nourishment of it,
aided by the grateful rain of kindness and

refinement, had made a lovely plant out of a hedgerow flower.

'Glad to see you back, Pat,' said Mr. Clavering; 'do you remember who that is?' he asked, pointing to Frank.

'I suppose it is your son, sir, if I may judge by his being so much like you,' answered Pat.

'You are quite right,' said Frank, rising to shake hands with his father's *protégé.*

'I am certain of it now, Mr. Clavering; I remember the voice perfectly well as the voice I heard in our cabin, and again on the day that Biddy led me up to Clonmore to play for you,' said the boy with a slight blush mantling his cheeks.

'You are not ashamed of those old days, Pat, are you?' asked Mr. Clavering.

'Not a bit, sir; rather proud of them,' replied Pat honestly.

' I'm glad to hear that, my boy ; you are a gentleman so long as you are not anxious to conceal where you came from, and one of *nature's* gentlemen, too, which are of the purest water. Now tell us something about the concert. Were there many people there ?'

' The room was full, sir ; there was some beautiful spinnet-playing, also playing on the harp and violin, and above all the voice of a lady, which was very sweet.'

' Who was it, Pat ?'

' I don't know, sir ; they told me that she was one of the best singers of the day, and then asked me if I would like to play for her to sing to. So I said " Yes." And she asked me very kindly if I liked something lively, or quiet and soft. I said, " Quiet, something to take us away out of the room and to carry us up to heaven."

"Oh," she said, "you are a poet, too, are you, Master O'Leary?" I answered that I was not, that I couldn't say what I meant, but I could play the thought for her. So I just played a little thing out of my head, and then she said, "You have great taste, my boy; perhaps this will suit you," and she put before me Handel's "Angels ever bright and fair;" and then she sang it as if she really saw the angels and felt her prayer. Then she said, "You must come to the Opera and hear me sing." I said, "I would be very glad to." So she called over a gentleman to her, and said to him, "I want you to let this gentleman accompany me in the leading airs next Wednesday night; will you allow him to do so?" "Oh yes," he said, "he may take a seat in the orchestra with pleasure; but you must let him have the score to practise." "He shall have that," she answered, "and shall practise them over with me just before." Then, turning to me, she said, "You will come and dine with me, my boy, will you not ?" I said, " Yes, if you would allow me." And she is going to send me the music to-morrow. She said a great deal about my playing. I do not play as well as she said I do; and as I was coming away, Sir Nugent Anson said to me, " Tell Mr. Clavering from me, that your fortune is made, because Madame —I do not recollect her name—has taken notice of you." '

' Was it Cavatini ?' asked Mr. Clavering.

' Yes, that was the name, sir ; they say she is the first singer of the day.'

' So she is, Pat ; and if, through her, you get an introduction to the musical world, your fortune is made. But do not accept

the place of first violin in the orchestra at
the Haymarket; you can do better than
that.   All I am anxious about is this, my
boy,' said Mr. Clavering earnestly, 'don't
let people turn your head with their
praises.'

'I do not think they will, sir,' replied
Pat simply.

'Do not be too sure of that, my boy;
wiser men than you or I have said the
same, and have toppled down from the
very pinnacle of honour in consequence,'
said Mr. Clavering sagaciously.

'I cannot take any praise to myself, sir.
In the first place, God gave me music
because I couldn't see; you or He—isn't
it ?—then made me see too, and thereby I
can play better now than I used to.   It is
no trouble to me to play, it is an easy
pleasure ; and so when people clap their

hands, I think they are praising the gift that I have, which belongs to God, though He has given it to me to take care of.'

'That is wisely said, Pat,' replied Mr. Clavering approvingly, 'and older heads might take a lesson from it. But take care that you always feel what you say, for there is very little worth in idle words which are no deeper than the throat. And now go to bed, my dear boy; you are tired, and you have your work cut out for you to do by next Wednesday. I will take a box at the Opera, and we will see if Miss O'Moore will not come too.'

When Pat had left the room, Mr. Clavering said:

'You are pleased with him, Frank, I hope; I cannot tell you what a link exists between that boy and me. I mean to keep him with us until I can send him off in a profession, which will be at no great distance of time. Really I do not wish to send him to live with his own class.'

'There is no reason why you should, father. If you are thinking of me, do not imagine for a moment that I have any objection to the boy's remaining in the house. It would be hard to turn him off now.'

'Well, I was just a little bit afraid, Frank, that you might object to him, but now that I have your assurance to the contrary, I am once more easy in mind, and will keep the boy with us until there is some opening for him.'

'How is it, father,' asked Frank, 'that there is so wide a difference between people that have risen from nothing? That boy will grow up a gentleman; and look what Lady O'Moore is like, certainly anything but a lady.'

'Yours is a difficult question to answer, Frank; but the difference seems to me to lie in this. Some of them have a gift from God, which must rise into life and greatness if they use it aright; such are, as a rule, humble and unpretentious and free from all affectation. But there are others, who, by a father's accident, are put into a position, or get it by their own scheming, as did Lady O'Moore, who have nothing to recommend them, no real worth or genius, and yet are pretentious, affect good family, practise all sorts of airs, and in fact are so unreal that they are easily seen through, and thus are easily known. Of course poor Sir Patrick's second wife added to these moral deficiencies and obliquities, and was utterly heartless.'

Here the conversation dropped.

The next day the music which Pat had

to practise was sent to him by his newly found friend and patroness the illustrious prima donna, together with a perfumed little note containing a box order for Mr. Clavering and his friends.

CHAPTER VII.

MUSIC AND HER SISTER SONG.

'Oh, two such silver currents, when they join,
Do glorify the banks that bound them in.'

PAT O'LEARY practised steadily at the
music sent to him by Madame Cavatini,
in which he was to take a part at the
Haymarket on the following Wednesday
night.

The opera was Mozart's 'Don Giovanni,'
which had been represented some twenty
years before for the first time, but which
had not yet been played in Paris.

This was, however, the first time that

Pat had seen the music of it, although he was already acquainted with ' Le Nozze di Figaro.'

As he went on with his practice, the more he entered into the spirit of the divine Mozart, and felt that his own best attempts at composition were but as shadows upon the sunlit fortress of the great composer's genius.

Some one has said that the opera of ' Don Giovanni ' has but one good *morceau*, and that is, its entire self.

But if Pat was delighted with the music as he learnt to play it as accompanist, and revelled in the ' La ci darem la mano ' and the ' Fui ch' han del mio,' what would he be when he heard the powerful and marvellous voice of Cavatini in ' Vedrai carino ?' and what would he do when he listened to her rendering of ' Batti, batti,

Masetto,' so beautifully given nowadays by Trebelli? But we must not anticipate his pleasure, but endeavour to share it with him when Wednesday night arrives.

Pat lived at a time which was not so rich in operas as our own; some of the best of them were written, it is true, but were not represented until long after the year of which we write. Even 'Don Giovanni' had been hissed off the stage at Vienna, in consequence of envy, aided by bad taste on the part of the public. Haydn alone was its champion at a reunion of *soi-disant* amateurs met for the purpose of criticising it, when he said, ' All that I know and am able to declare is this, that Mozart is the greatest composer of our day !'

The boy would by-and-by have the beauties of 'Il Flauto Magico' opened to

him ; 'Tancredi,' with its lovely cavatina
'Di tanti palpiti ;' 'Il Barbiere di Siviglia,'
that pearl of musical répertoire in our own
time and for all time, he would also live to
enjoy ; he would revel in ' Mosè in Egitto,'
and the magnificent overture to 'Semi-
ramis ;' it would fall to his lot to hear and
to play 'Guillaume Tell' and its lovely
cantabile for the violoncello, full of majesty,
and breathing in its melody the calm of
Alpine solitude ; as well as the 'Stabat
Mater' by the same mighty composer.
Later on he would hear 'Robert le Diable,'
'Les Huguenots,' 'Le Prophète ;' and
later still 'La Favorita,' 'Lucia di Lam-
mermoor,' 'La Figlia del Regimento,' and
'La Traviata,' and even the celebrated
' Faust,' written by one who still delights
thousands by his harmonious productions ;
but we doubt if Pat ever lived to put his

bow to his violin in order to join in with others in that exquisite *entr'acte* of 'La Colombe,' where notes follow one another in a succession of such exquisite delicacy that they sound even too gentle for the tread of fays upon blades of grass, and too hushed for a moonlight accompaniment to a dance of fairies' midsummer night's revel.

But *revenons à nos moutons.*

Wednesday evening arrived, and Pat set off with his violin, in its case, to dine with Madame Cavatini.

Kathleen O'Moore had consented, after some little pressure on Frank's part, to go to the Opera ; she had even gone so far as to lessen her mourning, and to promise to wear a crimson rose in her hair, which Frank Clavering had procured for her. He had only returned home a week ; his duties had occupied him the greater part of each day, and yet his father noticed a change in Kathleen for the better. She was less dead to her surroundings, and began to laugh a little when Frank told her anecdotes of the campaigns from which he had just returned.

Mr. Clavering was pleased beyond measure to see this spring, which might brighten into summer, after the long winter of sorrow that had chilled the poor girl's heart. He longed to see his son happy, and Frank would only be that when he could call Kathleen his wife. Would it ever come to pass? the affectionate father anxiously asked himself. There seemed to be some little chance of it now; so he did everything in his power to encourage Kathleen's spirits, and to enable her to shake off the past and to bring into her mind the idea that she must not despair of being happy yet.

But Kathleen would only shake her head, though she had to confess to herself that Frank's return had gone some way, even in a week's time, towards making her happier.

Frank was dressing for dinner, and Murphy, with military precision, in spite of having lost an arm, was assisting him.

'Well, Murphy,' he asked, 'how are you getting on ? Do you want to go back to Inchigeela?'

' I'm gettin' on right well, yer 'oner ; an' faith I like this much better than Clonmore, although I am constantly under fire,' replied the corporal.

' But there are no French here, Murphy ?'

' True enough, yer 'oner ; I niver caved

in to a Frenchman yet, although our whole rigiment showed a little bit of back at Talaveery an' Bisākus too ; but, faith, thin they were a thousand to one.'

'Who are you giving in to now, Murphy?' asked Frank, who had an idea what the campaign was of which his servant spoke. ' You have only been home a week, and you are giving in already.'

' Shure, sur, there's. bin a brisk fire goin' on the whole time from as bright a pair o' cannons as I ever set eyes on. They've turned me right wing, an' I've given in.'

' How do you mean, Murphy?' asked Frank, giving a last look at himself in the glass.

' Faith, yer 'oner, the inemy's called Green; an' I've come to terms wi' her, an' now we're goin' to be allied forces, for I've shown the flag of truce.'

'You have not been long about it, Murphy; I congratulate you though, for I hear that Mrs. Green has got a kind heart of her own as well as a pair of bright eyes. But what about Mrs. Machree?'

'Shure, I've niver considered her in the business. When you're refused once, that's enough for me, at any rate. An' Widdy Machree has lost her chance,' said Murphy, as he folded up a coat of his master's; 'she's the loser, poor sowl, not I.'

'Nothing like having a good opinion of yourself, Murphy,' said Frank, who was thinking how he himself had been once refused, but meant to renew the attack immediately. 'You must order the coach for a quarter to eight punctually.'

'Yes, yer 'oner; but plaise, have I yer consent to the marriage?' asked Murphy.

'My good man, I'm neither the bride's parent nor your own,' replied Frank; 'but of course you have my consent, and I hope you may be happy !'

By a concerted arrangement between Murphy and Mrs. Green, while the scene just related had been passing in Frank's room, another, similar in purport, had been enacted in Kathleen's room by the bride-elect; and thus, when Frank and Kathleen met in the drawing-room before dinner, they each had the same news for one another. Mr. Clavering laughed heartily, and made a remark that Murphy seemed to be as efficient a son of Venus as he had been of Mars; but he had no doubt that, with the warm hearts possessed by the two of them, it would be a marriage 'made in heaven.' He was about to say something concerning the close relationship

that would thus exist between Murphy
and the Countess Naufrancs; but he
stopped short, as he had too much feeling
for Kathleen to mention such a subject
before her, which might recall Hugh, whose
name, as has been said before, was buried
in the past.

Both Mr. Clavering and his son noticed
how well Kathleen was looking considering
her late troubles, and the former assured
his son that it was his return home which
had wrought the change in her. She was
dressed very becomingly that evening in
a black and grey costume, and wore the
rose in her hair which Frank had given
her.

While the two gentlemen were discussing
Kathleen over their smoking after dinner,
she was considering Frank in her own
mind in the drawing-room. The world

did not seem so dark to her now. Had
anyone told her a fortnight before this,
that Frank's return would make a pleasant
difference to her, she would have denied it
as a thing utterly impossible.   But she
found that she was happier than before
his return; she looked out anxiously for
him when he was away on business, and
she had to acknowledge to a sense of
inward relief when he had come home that
very evening from the War Office, and
informed her that he had not to go back
to the seat of war.   She reflected, and the
result of her reflection was more than
Byron's,

> ' Meditation bids us feel
> We once have loved ;'

for it showed her that she could, that she
did, love again.   But then, alas! her
thoughts wandered back to Hugh, and

for the first time since his death she
opened the locket which she wore round
her neck and looked upon his miniature.
That act recalled all; and when Mr.
Clavering and Frank entered the room to
tell her that the coach was at the door,
they found her pale and sad, while her
eyes were filled with tears, which she in
vain tried to conceal.

'Is anything wrong, dear Kathleen?'
asked Mr. Clavering.

'No, it is nothing. Is the coach come
round to the door yet?' she asked as com-
posedly as she could.

'Yes, it has,' answered Mr. Clavering,
who perceived that the locket lay open on
her neck; 'let me close this for you!' he
added.

Kathleen started and shut the little
locket quickly, but not before Mr. Claver-

ing had seen its contents, and rightly augured that it contained the reason for her tears.

Meanwhile Pat had been spending a pleasant two or three hours with Madame Cavatini. Before dinner they practised the two airs together sung by 'Zerlina'; these were all in which Pat would play a solo accompaniment for her. It was a fancy on the part of the *prima donna*, and an irregularity; but she overcame the latter by assuring the leader of the orchestra that she was 'out of voice,' and of course when the one to whom the filling of 'the house' was due expressed a wish, it was law.

Their work ended, madame and the Irish boy sat down to a *tête-à-tête* dinner in a charming little dining-room hung round with valuable prints; there was one of Garrick, another of Oliver Goldsmith, another of Mozart, while the mantelpiece and corner shelves were well filled with old and valuable china.

The *prima donna*, who had the kindest of hearts, made a great impression upon Pat, while he, in turn, had fascinated by his frank naïve manner the celebrated song-stress, who was a formidable rival to the nightingale in the richness and sweetness of her notes, and whose voice could be heard distinctly above the loudest accompaniment of the noisiest orchestra.

Pat gave an account of his life which interested his hostess, and he defined for her, as well as he could, the change from blindness to sight.

' How do you like " Don Giovanni ?" ' asked Madame Cavatini.

' Very much indeed,' answered Pat. ' I

thought it very beautiful when I played it over by myself, but I like it far better now that I have heard you sing it. How strange is the music when the statue walks in at the door after ' Don Giovanni ' has finished his supper ! It quite frightens me, but I so much want to see it.'

' Well, you will soon have that wish gratified. But come, my dear boy, you are thinking so much of what you have been playing and what you are going to listen to, that you are eating and drinking nothing. Have a little more of this chicken and a little more of that sherry wine ?' said the *prima donna.*

' No more, thank you,' answered Pat. ' Who is that over the fireplace ?' he asked, pointing in the direction of Oliver Gold-smith's portrait ; ' did he sing, or play, or make music ?'

'Dear me, no; he wrote poetry and one or two plays, and a story called the "Vicar of Wakefield." Didn't you ever hear of him before?' asked Madame Cavatini, resting a moment from the earnest plying of her knife and fork.

'No,' said Pat, 'I care for nothing and nobody not connected with music; do you?'

'Of course I do, my dear boy. I like music and musical people best, but it would be but a poor world and a very small one, if people had given up and still were to give up all their time to music. Where would America be if Columbus had been a fiddler at home, or what would become of Europe if Lord Wellington were a public singer?' asked madame.

'I do not know,' answered the boy, 'but I do not care for all that; give me music and trees and flowers, and I should be satisfied. I hope that heaven is all music.'

'Ah!' said Madame Cavatini, with a sigh, 'we cannot tell what that is like; but be sure that everything here is wisely distributed, and that there is neither too much nor too little of anything, except too much misery and unhappiness, and men have made that for themselves.'

Then Pat asked some questions about the old china, and his good-natured hostess told him how this was 'Sèvres' and that was 'blue Worcester,' and so on, until at length, when dinner was ended, she went off to dress, and left the boy some picture-books with which to entertain himself. But scarcely had she reached her room when she heard the sounds of a violin; then she smiled and thought to herself,

'Music is that child's only world, his value of it is perfectly uncorrupted; while I, and such as I, think too much, I am afraid, first of our début, then of our interpretations of different passages, and of public applause, losing sight of the music in ourselves. But he loses sight of himself in the music, and fancies that the world is set going by it, and that the stars are held in their places by means of it. He is innocent, dear boy; he doesn't know the world. Wait till he is my age; then he will look for applause, and will feel jealous if he thinks that his star is in any way declining, and that others can gather the laurels which he fancies belongs to his own wreath. Oh! the world is fickle; it is sham in its plaudits, and yet—it has behaved very well to me.'

At length the same 'world' had taken

their places in the Opera-house, and the house was crowded to excess. What a satire earthly enjoyment is! Fine dames and damsels were there for the purpose of pleasure, while perhaps the war in Spain had that very day laid low some of their dearest ones, on whose faces they would never look again.

For the one, the bitterness of death was past; for the other, the grief which it brings along with its sable train had yet to come. 'Hodie mihi cras tibi!' truthfully stands written over the gate of a cemetery in the far East. But it is not with the world as a stage that we have to do at present; it is with the stage proper.

Mr. Clavering, Kathleen, and Frank were in their box, with their six eyes fixed on Pat, who in turn saw his friends, and made a sign to them with his 'bow.'

At length the bell sounded, the orchestra struck up the overture, and Pat was soon heart and soul in his music. The leader watched the boy, and turned his ear to catch the strains that came from his violin; but he listened in vain for a false note, and surveyed with pleasure the intense interest which shone on the youthful face.

The curtain rose upon the well-known opening scene of 'Don Giovanni.' The air of Leporello, 'Notte e giorno,' was well rendered, and so was the scene of the death of the Commander. Donna Maria's accents of sorrow were given with great feeling, and the trio 'Ah! chi mi dice.'

Pat was overjoyed with the performance as it went on, and knew his music so well that he was able to keep his eyes fixed upon the stage, thus enhancing the mean-ing of the music and the wonderful connec-

tion between the libretto and the score
in his own mind.

The air ' Madamina il catalogo' and the
celebrated duet were ended, and Pat's
especial task came on. Cavatini, if she
were really 'out of voice,' as she said, yet
sang splendidly. 'Vedrai carino' was ex-
quisitely given, and the accompaniment,
guided by the signs of the *prima donna*
was all that could be desired. It was
rapturously encored. But when ' Batti,
batti, Masetto' was finished, an encore
did not suffice, so Cavatini had to sing it a
third time, amid a shower of applause and
bouquets, one of which fell from Mr.
Clavering's box, and was acknowledged
by a graceful curtsey.

Pat's interest never flagged until the end
of the opera. The flush of excitement
mantled upon his cheek, and many were

the fair eyes which regarded the handsome boy, and did not fail to remark his enthusiasm or the fact of his accompanying, as soloist, the great *prima donna*.

And what had been taking place in the box occupied by Mr. Clavering?

Mr. Clavering himself felt proud of his *protégé's* success, and his eyes dwelt affectionately on the boy's fair head. Once or twice he left the box for the professed purpose of taking air in the passage, but in reality to let Frank and Kathleen talk alone and uninterrupted. He had noticed that they seemed to be greatly interested in one another, more so than they had ever been within his recollection. Was his fond desire to be realised at last? If so, he would not thwart it by being *de trop*.

But little passed between the two young

people that evening. Once Frank took a tiny hand in his own and said :

'Kathleen, do you remember what I once used to say ?'

'Yes, Frank,' was the answer given with downcast eyes.

'What have you to say about it now ?' asked Frank.

'Only that I love you now, and I never did that long ago,' was the reply.

Frank raised the little hand to his lips, for he was content.

CHAPTER VIII.

A FLIGHT IN WINTER.

'There's a divinity that shapes our ends,
Rough-hew them how we will.'

COUNTESS NAUFRANCS' married life was
slipping by. It had begun in March; it
wanted now only a week to Christmas
Day. Pleasure and happiness speed time,
but sorrow and disappointment and care
clog its wings and make it a burden instead
of a swift-passing boon. And surely no
months should pass so speedily, or be so
regretted when gone, as the first few
months of married life; surely no hours

or days should run so smoothly as those which make them up, no matter what the time of year—spring, summer, autumn, or winter.   Yet it is not the fact of marriage, but the motive of marriage, which speeds the days and tints them with rose-colour. A situation may be delightful of itself, but not in its circumstances; Portland may be charming, but not if your circumstances confine you within its prison walls; a sea voyage may be most invigorating and expanding, but not if your circumstances place you on board an emigrant ship, and you are tightly packed in 'between decks' among boxes and bedding and wrangling women and screaming children.   So with marriage; the meaning of marriage, the situation of marriage, is delightful of itself, but not if its circumstances are guided and controlled and continued and carried out in and under the wrong motives which brought it about. It is love, true and pure and holy, which is its only acceptable motive, and which alone can make the days short and happy and too few; all other motives, whatever they be—intrigue, money, or ambition—make marriage a burden grievous to be borne.

And 'thus it befell Countess Naufrancs. Her first marriage, as marriage, had been irksome to her; that is to say, she found no pleasure in her husband's company. Sir Patrick had loved her, and was therefore kind and considerate and indulging; so nothing clashed: her worldliness had grated upon him, but his goodness had satisfied her. But in her second marriage her lot was very different. Two currents met, both strong, but one stronger and fiercer than the other; and so much stronger and fiercer that it had its own way in the end, and carried everything along in its selfish swamping course.

The few months of her second married life wrought wonders in the before-unscathed person of Lady O'Moore, in the careless, heartless woman who sought her own ends, and laid aside love as needless and natural affection as an obstacle which came in the way of pleasure.

All had been sacrificed for self; all might have come to grief unheeded and unwept for, so far as she was concerned, save herself. But now she was attacked in a manner too ferocious for resistance, and the shrine of her favourite deity, Herself, was being ruthlessly destroyed under the cruel mercenary reign of a heartless tyrant.

There were traces to be seen now of

sorrow and care. The hair was silvered, the eyes were dimmed, the head was bowed, and the cheek was sunken and blanched. The toilette was neglected, and all effort to keep up appearances had died away.

Never had the destruction of a temple of Baal nor the plunder of a shrine of Ashtaroth, nor the desecration of a moonlit grotto of Diana, nor the violation of a perfumed garden or a fern-grown glade of Flora, occasioned respective devotees such keen sorrow and loud lamentation as did the destruction of Lucy, Countess Nau-francs occasion herself. She was a temple reared by much labour; she was not a sudden creation; her growth had been gradual, and it had been fostered with great care. She had schemed from the laying of the foundation-stone until the

gilding of the vane.   But alas! it was not
the finishing touch which held the building
together; it was not the gilt which could
withstand the storm : the foundation alone
could have done that, but even it was
unequal to the task.   It had never been
securely laid.   There had never been a
gift of love upon her altar; the gifts placed
thereon were neither sanctified by the altar
nor by the temple.   She had been temple,
altar, Deity, and worshipper; and should
an idolatry to bow down to itself, it will be
found, at length, like Dagon in days of
old, lying upon its face in its own temple,
broken to pieces.   She had imagined
herself perfect; she had been proud of
what she had reared; she never considered
the possibility of a fall, so that when it
came, it came intensified by non-expectation
and by unreadiness to meet it.

It is the old, old story of 'a house built upon the sand,' and such old, old stories as that cannot be repeated too often, for they grasp with the consciousness of a few lines what human intellect cannot so well or so completely explain in the largest volume that was ever written.

The countess bore as long as she could with the insatiable avarice and the ceaseless cruelty of the man she had married. There was no end to his demands, and her five hundred a year seemed nothing. She could not touch her capital, but she was compelled to borrow upon it, and had already done so to the extent of four years ahead, and therefore to the amount of two thousand pounds. Scarcely a penny had she to spend upon herself; but this did not trouble her, she scarcely paid attention to the necessaries of life. The money did not worry her; she would have slaved for more, she would have cringed to Kathleen for more, in return for some little sympathy and love. It was the brutality that told upon her. The count had of late been fortunate at 'play'; that did not lessen his avarice. His cry always was 'Give me more;' and the more he got, the more he wanted.

The countess had long since given up entertaining; she had neither the spirit nor the opportunity for receiving friends. Her carriage was sold, so were her dresses and laces and furs. The number of her retinue was reduced from six to one, who was just a general servant; one who in aspect and occupation must have vividly recalled household arrangements of the countess's childhood. Mrs. Rouse, her housekeeper, had been faithful enough so

long as there was wealth ; but when this
went, Mrs. Rouse went too, carrying off
all such booty as had been given her, and
a good deal more that she had given herself. And why should Mrs. Rouse be
blamed ? Is it not the way of the world ?
Rich to-day, plenty of friends, friends who
will come to see you twenty times a day ;
friends who will generously drink your
wine, partake of your hospitality, ride your
horses, and drive in your carriages ; you
are most popular, in fact the idol of a
large circle. And yet it is not yourself
that attracts ; it is what you have. And
this can easily be proved by looking at
another aspect of yourself. You are still
yourself, you still possess the same amiable
qualities, you still have the same faults,
but you have lost your money. How
many friends have you ? How many are

there who express sympathy with you in your misfortune? how many are there who will cross the road to shake hands with you? how many who will say a word of extenuation because you have left debts unpaid which they helped to pile up for you? How many? Perhaps one or two, but no more. Rich to-day, plenty of friends; poor and down-trodden to-morrow, and not one to raise you from the gutter, or to say a good word when others abuse you. Money is the root of much friendship, as it is the root of all evil. Mrs. Rouse, then, was no worse than the rest of the world.

Count Naufrancs was no teetotaler. In France he had imbibed quantity, but not quality so far as strength went. 'Vin de Bordeaux,' 'anisette,' and 'eau sucré' were very harmless in their way, and not inebriating. But when he came to England and began to take an equal quantity of stronger beverages, the result was evident. His head was not strong, and his temper was easily excited, and the consequence was that both were very much affected ; he lost the one and the other. He always accepted an invitation to *prendre quelque chose*, and it was not often that his French-speaking acquaintances had to say to him, *Buvez donc, mon cher;* or to remark, *Tu ne bois n'en.*

On a certain night he returned home after losing money, head and temper at a debauch.

His wife had been sitting before the fire in her room waiting up for him. Yes, waiting up *for him;* she would do anything now for a kind word or a smile, anything to produce the one or to provoke the other; she would even cringe and fawn and flatter. But it was all in vain; her little attentions were only cursed at, and even did she throw herself at his feet, she was only spurned with his foot. Poor Lucy! Is there then no one to pity you as you sit before the fire? Is there no one who will put a tender arm about your neck, or push back the hair from your fevered forehead, or wipe the burning tear from your pale wan face? Is there no one among the living who will do this for you? Is there no one of your late friends who will even breathe a word of comfort in your ear? Is there no living soul to help you? Where are your thoughts now? All in the past all meshed and netted in the sunshine of the past, recalling this or that pleasure, this or that fascination and joy! And whither do they turn again? To the living? No, to the dead; and not to them as they are, but as they were; wishing, oh! so earnestly, for the dear good husband and his great unselfish love, for the little innocent babe who died upon its cradle death-bed without a mother's presence. Oh for the one now to support you and to comfort you! oh for the other to clamber up upon your knee, to entwine its babyish arms about your neck, and to ask you in lisping accents why you weep! But they have both left you, they have both gone beyond the grave; and they cannot return to you, although you may go to them. And your thoughts are now back to the time when they brought your dying husband home from the hunting-field, and when they brought you the news of your little one's

death.   How heartless you were then, and
how you regret it now !

She had let the fire burn low in her sad
thinking, and it was now little more than
embers.   But suddenly she started from
her seat, for she heard uncertain steps
upon the stairs.   She threw back the hair
from her throbbing temples, gave a look in
the mirror at her wan face, and at her eyes
red from weeping, and tried to bring the
look of a welcome into her face.   What
an unreality, what a mockery it was ! she
loathed the man at her heart, and yet she
would stoop very low now for a kind word,
and even from him.   She heard his mutter-
ings, she had her misgivings, but she faced
the door of the room, her heart beating
violently.   A moment afterwards the door
was thrown violently open, and her
husband entered.   There was a madness

in his eye, and his whole appearance was so threatening and ferocious that the woman trembled.

'You ——!' he muttered, 'you've let the fire out, and I'm as cold as ice.'

He raised his hand, struck her savagely, and she fell beneath the weight of the blow. Then he raised her in his arms and thrust her out into the passage. There she lay for some time stunned and quite unconscious. At length she came to her senses. She rose wearily to her feet, passed her hand across her forehead, and went towards the door of her room. She listened a moment and heard the heavy breathing of her sleeping maudlin husband. She stopped for a moment or two, hesitating as to what step she should take next. If she waited until to-morrow, he would continue his persecution of her; to-morrow only meant more cruelty and extortion, and more pain and misery for herself. Why should she brook such treatment any longer? Who was there now to notice whether she lived with her husband or whether she left him? All her friends had gone with the days that were departed. She was neglected, and she longed for peace. Oh! how differently would she act if she could live her time over again! But there was no use in these vain regrets; the question to be decided was, should she go or should she stay? She decided to go, to go and never to return.

She crept downstairs noiselessly to the door, and went out into the cold night. She had an object in view as she went along the streets. She drew the shawl over her head which lay around her shoulders, and walked quickly until she reached the outskirts of the town and left the city behind her. But she did not yet stay her hurrying feet. On, on, she hastened, ever and anon looking back to see that no one was in pursuit, for she feared that her husband would follow her when he awoke and discovered that she had left home. Home indeed! it was a place of suffering to her, and that was all.

Out into the country by a muddy road she pursued her way. Her shoes were soaking wet, she was chilled through and through, she paused a moment to think upon and to try and realise what she was doing.

Could this be herself? Was this the end of her scheming and her self-pride, and the satisfaction she was to reap from a life which was always striving for more?

Was this the summit of her ambition? All her desire for pleasure and gaiety were past; to-morrow was without anticipation. She longed only for quiet, and she fancied she might get that at the new home she was seeking.

She hurried on, and at length stopped before a high door in a garden wall, and pulled a long iron bell-handle. While she is waiting for an answer and for admission, we will retrace our steps a little and go back to see the cause and object of this midnight visit.

It was about three months before this that Sister Theresa, of a Carmelite order of nuns, had called upon the countess, who had become a Catholic upon her marriage with Sir Patrick O'Moore. Was it from conscientious motives? or was it because poor Sir Patrick had been a sturdy

Catholic and might have had objections to marrying a Protestant? We forbear to inquire.

Sister Theresa was not a wily Roman; she was devout, charitable, and sincere. She had no doubts about her faith; she was willing blindly to accept all that her Church might teach, however untenable it might appear to her common-sense or however hard to her conscience. She had called upon the countess, in company with another of her order, for the purpose of begging on behalf of the poor who would sorely need assistance for the then approaching winter. The countess had responded liberally to her appeal, and more than this, had been struck by the quiet atmosphere which seemed to surround the sister's person and by the calm content of her demeanour. She had asked

Sister Theresa to call again, and the sister had done so. She found comfort in her peaceful society, and she neither restrained her tears nor masked her sorrows before her.

Again and again the sister came; the countess told her all; her past history, her worldly aims, and finally the unhappy state to which her second marriage had reduced her.

Her ladyship also mentioned that she had five hundred a year until her death. Is it a wonder if a sister, anxious for the support of her own sisterhood, pressed home to the lady the emptiness of this world and the deceitfulness of riches, and displayed an anxiety on behalf of her spiritual welfare? 'A little leaven leaveneth the whole lump,' and five hundred a year added to the resources of a convent is an addition if it is nothing else.

'Ah! madame,' said the sincere sister, with one eye fixed on her creed and another on the shadowy certainty of five hundred a year, 'you cannot tell how weary is this world, how vain are its cares and empty its pleasures, until you leave it! I have found that. Within the cloister there is indeed peace, there is the satisfaction of living a pure and unspotted life; if you ever want peace come thither, and when you have once entered the garden-gate your sorrows will be left outside, and the peace of eternity will enter your soul.'

And this little speech, made in sincerity, mistaken though it may have been in its idea of perfect peace being anywhere in this world, had left its impression upon the countess's mind.

Is there perfect peace in the cloister for all? Has it not, too, its petty strifes and divisions, its disappointments and its ambitions? Surely it is those alone who go there from feelings of earnest conviction and a heartfelt determination to live purely or to work for others who find the peace they hoped to find. Those who enter without such motives find more peace, far more peace in the world than in the religious life.

But we left the countess waiting for admission at the gate of the Convent of our Lady of Carmel. She rang twice before anyone came to the gate; then someone looked through a small grating and asked, ' Who is there ?'

' Let me in for the sake of heaven and our Lady's pity; I am the Countess Naufrancs, and I am come to cast in my lot with yours. I must see Sister Theresa.'

There was the jingle of keys, the noise of the fitting of a key into a lock, and the door opened to admit the countess. She entered, and it was shut behind her. Peace! was it to be peace?

She was conducted into a little waiting-room within the convent. It was simple and neat.

In a few moments Sister Theresa entered; there was an affectionate greeting between the sister and her ladyship, and the object of the visit was explained. About a week after this, Countess Naufrancs renounced the pomps and vanities of this wicked world, and took her religious names, Ursula-Maria. The count had endeavoured to find out the retreat of his unhappy wife, but his search had been in vain.

We must now take leave of Sister
Ursula, but before doing so, let us take
a final glance at her and her situation.

*   *   *   *   *

It is the last day of the old year. Many
years have passed by since the night that
Sister Ursula entered the convent. She is
sitting in the convent library. The wintry
sun is setting, and its rays are coming in
at the window across the terraced garden.
She has been repairing books ; some old
volumes of religious lore or of ignorant
bigotry. Her work is laid aside, and soon
the ' Ave Maria ' will ring out, and she
with others will join her voice to praise the
Virgin Mother. The old sister, for she is
old now, goes out through the library
window upon the garden terrace. In
summer it is gay with many little flowers,
heartsease and roses bloom in the beds,

and pure lilies blossom in the quaint old flower-pots upon the stone balcony. But now there are only a few bare stalks or a few hardy plants that can bear the wintry weather.

At the end of the terrace there is a babbling little fountain. It is cool and pleasant in summer, but now seems chilly and uninviting. Above it is a niche, with an image of our Lady of Carmel; and above that again, a wicker cage once tenanted by a blackbird. Sister Ursula walks slowly down the terrace towards the fountain. One of the convent servants, an old gardener, stands there leaning upon his broom, with which he has been tidying the terrace and robbing it of its dead leaves.

The man takes off his hat reverently to the old sister.

'Another year nearly gone, Joseph,' said Sister Ursula; 'the sun has just set for ever upon this year.'

'Yes, sister,' replied the man; 'the five-and-fortieth year of my service here, and it all seems short enough, too.'

'The five-and-twentieth of my sister-hood, Joseph, and it has seemed weary and long. Would that the sun might never rise upon me again! I am very tired of this life, and quite ready to leave it. I have just about as much pleasure in existence as those dead leaves you have been brushing up. They seemed crushed and faded and wearied enough, and so am I. I was once as fresh and as happy as they were, flickering in the sun-shine.'

'Why, Sister Ursula,' said a cheery voice behind her, 'it is not often *you* are out in the garden. You have chosen a wintry day, too, when all looks withered and sad. There was no getting you out in the summer.'

The voice was that of the Mother Superior, of a woman older than Sister Ursula, but it was clear and bright. She had an intelligent and benevolent face, a face that spoke of earnest devotion and of a past life of purity and self-denial, and it seemed as though some reflection of Paradise, in which she so much coveted a share, already shone in her face.

' Cheer up, Sister Ursula,' she continued, ' cheer up, dear one! Be happy in God and Mary, and do not let sad thoughts of the past be always dwelling in your mind.'

' It is not that, mother,' replied the other ; ' I am old and ill.'

'And nearer to heaven for that, Ursula,' said the superior kindly, laying her hand upon the sister's arm. 'But it is chilly; come into my room for a few minutes and sit by the fire. The " Angelus " will ring presently.'

Very different women were the superior of the convent and Sister Ursula. The one had been within the cloister all her life, or nearly so, and had led a life of quiet unobtrusive piety and self-denial, first as a 'novice,' then as a 'professed,' then as 'superior of the convent.' The life had been very beautiful, so peaceful and yet so helpful and directing; it had instilled itself with its quiet ways and gentleness into other members of the convent, who, following the example never thrust upon them, became gentle, self-denying, and unworldly, living in the happiness of

doing good, shut out from the world, leading a pious life, though perhaps in a mistaken way.

But with Sister Ursula the past and
present were very different. As we know,
she had sought the cloister as a relief from
the strife of the world outside, and though
her prayers seemed earnest and her self-
denial great and her life saint-like from
every point of view, yet superior and
sisters saw, although the routine was gone
through, that the thoughts were often sad
and dreary and far away. They told her,
but in vain, to banish her evil thoughts,
and to remember that this world is not for
aye.

She knew that; she neither regretted
the present nor looked on to the future,
but sadly sorrowed over what was past;
and it was thinking of the past which made

her long to die, for in death she fancied
there might be forgetfulness. It was a sad
ending to a grasping life. She had none
of the simple faith of the sisters around
her. She had known the world and loved
it, while most of them had never tasted of
its sweet or bitter fruit.

But to return to the superior's room. It
was poorly furnished, yet scrupulously
clean. There were a few signs of taste
about it. Taste in a sister's cell! Yes,
there is such a thing as that, though one
might not find it in the cell of a Trappist.
There were touches of refinement here and
there; here some old faded books in
morocco leather, their once gilt edges now
black with age; there an antique vase which
had represented upon its base some scene
in the mythology of ancient Rome. Upon
the walls were a few pictures by an un-

known hand, but of undoubted merit ; and hanging over the mantelpiece was a cambric handkerchief edged with lace, but discoloured with dust and age. It was evidently some relic.

'I have often wondered what that little handkerchief means,' said Sister Ursula ; 'may I ask ?'

'The once owner of it is not far off,' said the mother, taking it down from the nail on which it hung and handing it to the sister. 'Do you recognise the initials ?'

'I do,' said Sister Ursula ; 'that was mine when I was Lucy O'Moore. Oh,' she sobbed, 'will He ever forgive me for the way in which I treated that husband and that babe He gave into my keeping ? He never can ; I do not deserve forgiveness !'

'Hush ! hush! Ursula,' said the mother compassionately, as she drew the sobbing sister towards her; 'you know that He forgave even the Magdalene.'

CHAPTER IX.

KINGSBOROUGH.

'Il segreto per esser felice.'

FRANK'S contentment, mentioned at the conclusion of a previous chapter, was not permanent; it was only for the time being, and until he might receive something better than the mere assurance of affection. He did not, however, go straight to the point, but waited his time for Kathleen's sake as well as his own. He knew that her nature had received a great shock, and he did not wish to impair or impede her recovery by thrusting too suddenly upon her the request he longed to make, hard as he found it to restrain himself.

Kathleen had at length acknowledged that she loved him ; that was a step towards marriage, and a nearer step than she had ever taken before. Even in the days of long ago, those school-days passed at Inchigeela, under the rule of Mistress O'Brien, Kathleen had only liked her playmate, and had been fickle and perverse, and such had been her character when she bade adieu to Frank before he left for the Peninsula.

But now that was changed, and in the place of light uncertainty there was sober-mindedness and fixity of purpose brought about in the school of affliction, that great moulder of character.

No schoolmistress or governess could

have taught her so well as sorrow had done, that life is not a season for jest and carelessness, but is a time of serious preparation and of stern reality.

We live and learn, and a life of trouble does more for our character and our sincerity than would a life of pleasure and of freedom from care. It is the living through hostile circumstances that makes men and women of us, that gives us muscle and the power to say 'no'; we become hardy plants, and can stand all weathers; whereas if the tender exotic be brought out from the conservatory into the cold air, it withers and dies.

Trouble braces up our nerves, though it silvers or whitens our hair; it gives us heart, it teaches us sympathy, and, taking us out of the narrow world of self and out of the prison of egotistic opinion, enables us to look upon others and their particular views in a more liberal and rational light.

Christmas Day came round to our friends in London, and it brought for Mr. Clavering a letter from Sister Ursula of the Carmelite order of nuns.

He recognised the writing, but the address and signature filled him with surprise. As he read the letter his thoughts for the writer changed to pity, and he felt that she was now paying the penalty of her past sins. He handed the letter to his son to read, but he contented himself by informing Kathleen that her stepmother had entered a convent in order to end her days in peace.

This intelligence surprised Kathleen, but she asked no questions, although she rightly argued within herself that her stepmother's second marriage had proved unhappy, and that this was therefore sufficient reason for her seclusion.

Two days before this the lower regions of Mr. Clavering's house had been festive over the nuptial rites of Murphy and Mrs. Green.

The former had been magnificent in his attire, and the bouquet worn in his button-hole, and the figured waistcoat of silk, which were the most prominent features in his toilette, were beyond description. Frank had in vain offered him a suit of quiet well-made clothes; Murphy's remark was that a man's wedding was 'of rare occurrence,' and that therefore his costume should be 'distinguished,' and out of the common.

Mr. Clavering and his son were unable to restrain their laughter when Murphy made his appearance before his departure for church to be married; but at the same time they admired the quiet pretty way in which Mrs. Green was dressed, thanks to the taste of Kathleen as *modiste,* and to the fact that Mrs. Green had been amenable to her young mistress's ideas upon the subject of dress, and had shut her ears to Murphy's importunities to put 'a little bit o' colour here and there.'

After the wedding breakfast, the hilarity of which reached the ears of those upstairs, Mr. and Mrs. Murphy were despatched to take their honeymoon some few miles from town.

There was a double object in this honeymoon; it was partly to afford a retreat for the newly-married couple, and partly that Murphy and his wife might superintend the warming of a new house built and furnished by Mr. Clavering some twenty miles from London.

'The Glen,' as the new house was called, had been built without the knowledge of Frank or of Kathleen. Pat O'Leary was aware of the work which had been going on, and had paid several visits with Mr. Clavering to the scene of the building at Kingsborough, a place close to the sea.

Mr. and Mrs. Murphy did not know whither they were going; their trip had been arranged by Mr. Clavering himself, and he had merely given the couple orders to warm the house thoroughly, as he, Mr. Frank, and Miss Kathleen, would be down by New Year's Day.

Mr. Clavering's idea was to give the residence to Frank and Kathleen as a wedding-gift, should they consent to marry one another. He had really built the cote before he had the two doves to put into it; but he was pretty certain, from the proceedings of the last three or four months, that when Kathleen was asked to become Frank's wife she would consent.

'The Glen' was a handsome house, built of brick, and was beautifully situated. Mr. Clavering had spent a large sum on its erection and on the furnishing of it, but he felt that he could not devote too much money to the happiness of the son whom he dearly loved, or of her whom he already regarded in the light of a daughter.

In building this house it turned out that Mr. Clavering had not acted hastily. It wanted but an hour to dinner on Christmas Day. He was sitting before the fire in his own room when Frank entered.

'Father,' he said excitedly, 'I have good news for you; Kathleen has consented to become my wife.'

'My dear, dear boy,' said Mr. Clavering affectionately, taking him by both hands, 'I congratulate you; I feel the joy of this good fortune only second to yourself. Where is Kathleen? I must go and see her. I knew that all would come right in the end. But come along to Kathleen!'

The young lady was soon discovered, and received Mr. Clavering's congratulations with a good many blushes, but with happiness evident upon her face.

'May God bless this union!' said Mr. Clavering fervently; 'this is the happiest day of my life!'

And when they gathered in the drawing-room before dinner, every face was radiant with pleasure.

Several intimate friends were invited to share Mr. Clavering's hospitality that evening, and among them, Pat O'Leary's friend Madame Cavatini.

It was a merry party which gathered round their host's well-furnished board. The news of Kathleen's engagement soon circulated among the guests, and there was a twinkle of participation in the happy event of the day in the eyes of all.

The curtains were drawn close, the fire burnt cheerily in its grate, and the dining-room was a little world of comfort, peopled by warm and loving hearts.

And the event commemorated was not forgotten, but remembered, as the celebration of the birth of Him 'who loveth us and gave Himself for us.'

On such occasions as this do not let us imagine that our warm home is a reflection of the outside world. We may have food enough, or too much, but let us remember that outside the windows, perhaps on our very door-step, there is some poor creature starving and perishing of cold.

A shilling or a few crumbs will go a long way, and we are indeed misinterpreting the spirit of the birthday we celebrate, if, in the enjoyment of our own social circle and cosy fireside, we forget the poor and needy who are spiritually our sharers in the blessing which came down from heaven on this holy day.

After dinner, when the cloth was removed, according to the custom of those good old days, and the dessert was placed upon the shining mahogany table, one of the guests stood up in his place, and Frank

room before dinner, every face
with pleasure.

Several intimate friends were
share Mr. Clavering's hosp:
evening, and among them, Pat
friend Madame Cavatini.

It was a merry party whicl
round their host's well-furnis!
The news of Kathleen's engag∈
circulated among the guests,
was a twinkle of participatic
happy event of the day in the e∋

The curtains we
burnt cheerily
room was
by war

umstances, to
deferred the
is happiness
1," they say,
ut when such
e pleasure is
ny dear boy
; he is a man
e an untruth,
steel. I love
own and her
:ant prayer is
and the other
or eternity.'
) his feet and
the **evening**

and Kathleen, who looked at one another, knew what was coming.

Mr. Ford, who had risen to propose a toast, was a bachelor some seventy-five winters old, and a brother-in-law to Mr. Clavering. He was old-fashioned in dress, and antique in manner, but his face bore the mark of perfect good-nature. His hair was white, and his countenance ruddy— 'ruddier than the cherry'—in consequence, *possibly*, of the heat of the room; we dare not suspect anything else, for we all know how abstemious our fathers were at the beginning of this century, and how much water they drank.

'Permit me, ladies and gentlemen,' he said, 'to call your attention to a subject, or rather to two subjects, which I have before me. The one is a lady, I cannot possibly enter upon her feelings, never having been a member of her sex; the other is a gentleman, and though I pride myself upon being another, yet such feelings as he must now entertain have never come within the range of my experience.

' My heart has never been wounded by such a power as has wounded the hearts of the two subjects under contemplation and consideration, and perhaps some one may say, and with truth, that I have no right to speak upon subjects upon which I am ignorant, and more than this, upon subjects of which I confess my ignorance. So far, such a piece of advice would hold good. But I am coming to a part of the subject on which I *may* express my opinion, and in which opinion you will agree with me. I am not heartless, ladies and gentlemen, though I have but one heart in keeping; nevertheless, that heart is whole. I cannot look upon suffering unmoved, nor can I pass it by without endeavouring to alleviate it. Remember, I do not consider that the two subjects before me are suffering ; I am coming to my point presently. No more can I see another happy without expressing my satisfaction at his happiness, nor without feeling happy in his happiness. Now the two subjects having resolved to blend themselves into one, and two paragraphs having decided to become one paragraph, without stops, has occasioned much happiness to my dear time-honoured friend Mr. Cecil Clavering. To be open, ladies and gentlemen, Miss O'Moore, daughter, by the way, of another dear warm-hearted friend of mine in days long ago, has consented to become Mrs. Francis Clavering. I rejoice at this, because it occasions

my friend, our kind host, the greatest
pleasure. No one deserves happiness
more than he does, for there never lived
a more conscientious, a more warm-hearted
or truer man, than my friend. It is many,
many years ago now since I was present
at his own wedding, and I can only hope
and pray that his son may find in his wife
the sterling qualities and goodness that his
father found in my dear and youngest
sister. But we must be cheerful and not
sad,' continued the kind-hearted old man,
as he brushed away a tear with the back
of his hand; 'and I ask you to drink to
the health of our kind host, and of his
beloved son and future daughter-in-law.
I am'a poor orator, ladies and gentlemen,
perhaps because I am no Irishman; I
cannot speak one twentieth part as well
as Madame Cavatini will sing for us after

dinner,' he added with a knowing laugh, 'but I ask one and all to drink to the long life and happiness of Mr. Cecil Clavering, his son Frank, and Miss O'Moore.'

The toast was warmly responded to, and Mr. Clavering replied in a very few words as follows; he was much affected by the reference which had been made to his late wife.

'Ladies and gentlemen, I thank you on behalf of my son and Miss O'Moore, and also on behalf of myself, for the kind manner in which you have responded to my dear friend and brother-in-law's toast. I do not deserve all he has said for me, but he was indeed right in supposing that this is a very happy day for me. Since my dear son was a very small boy, I wished him nothing better than to marry Kathleen O'Moore; it has all along been his desire to do so, but circumstances, to which I will not refer, have deferred the almost consummation of his happiness until now. "Hope deferred," they say, "maketh the heart sick," but when such a hope is realised, then the pleasure is intense. I am proud of my dear boy Frank, ladies and gentlemen; he is a man of honour, he never told me an untruth, he is brave and true as steel. I love Kathleen O'Moore for her own and her father's sake, and my constant prayer is and will be that the one and the other may be happy for now and for eternity.'

After this Frank rose to his feet and said a few words. The rest of the evening passed very merrily; everyone was happy under the influence of their kind-hearted host. Madame Cavatini favoured the company with one or two songs, Pat played her accompaniments, and also played one or two solos, and one or two duets with Kathleen, she performing on the harp. The company did not disperse until after midnight.

The next day Mr. Clavering wrote to Murphy, saying that his visit to 'The Glen' was postponed, but to have all in readiness.

The marriage was arranged to take place in February. The time went too slowly for Frank, until at length the happy day arrived and Kathleen became his wife.

This happiness had been long waited for ; at one time it seemed impossible, but now that the dearest wish of his heart was realised, he felt as though all that had transpired had not only been for the best, but had rendered his present possession more worth the having.

And on the night before the wedding, Mr. Clavering had handed over 'The Glen' to his son as a wedding gift. What a surprise it was to Frank, and how the father enjoyed that surprise, saying as he did at the time, 'All I have is yours, my dear boy, you know that; but I wanted to get ready a little surprise for you, and a place where you might live comfortably. I hope you will like it; I built it before I had anyone for certain to put into it. Murphy has been there two months getting it aired for you; and mind, I shall expect an invitation down as soon as you care to see me.'

It is needless to say how they at once expressed the hope of seeing him down very shortly.

The bride and bridegroom were en-chanted with 'The Glen.' It far surpassed their expectations, both as regards size and situation and finish.

Murphy was installed with all the conscious pride of major-domo. They were delighted with everything, while their hearts were deeply touched at the thoughtful and self-denying love of the man whose greatest happiness consisted in making and seeing other people happy.

One little incident touched Kathleen very deeply. It was this. Over the sideboard in the dining-room hung a life-like, life-size portrait of her father attired in hunting-dress. It recalled forcibly days long ago, and all the pleasure and trouble of the past rushed upon her in an instant, and it was some little time before she could recover her self-possession.

It was no wonder, as Murphy said, 'that Mistress Claverin' should take on so,' for when he came into the house and into the dining-room for the first time, he thought 'Sir Patrick was goin' to spaike to him.'

It was not long before Mr. Clavering received a pressing letter from his son begging him to come down at once and pay a visit, not forgetting to bring Pat with him.

The invitation was readily accepted, and the happiest days of the father's life were passed at 'The Glen,' in the consciousness that his only son was truly happy.

Patrick O'Leary found a friend in Frank's next-door neighbour, a lady of title, Lady Isabelle Clynton, the eldest daughter of the fifth Earl of Duchesney.

She was descended from a very old family which came over with the Conqueror; the only misfortune about it was this, that the family left all their money

behind them in Normandy and never made
any in England.   But there was the title,
and that had been enough for Mr. Julius
Clynton ; he had plenty of money himself,
and was content to take the Lady Isabelle
without any dowry, although she brought
him a good many manuscripts of her own
composit on, which had been the round of
the London magazines, and were in most
cases rejected.   With some of her compositions she had, however, been more fortunate, and Lady Isabelle Clynton was
known as the authoress of 'The Brush of
an Angel's Wings,' 'The Moonlit Firs,' and
so on.   She was always bewailing to herself that she was not more appreciated by
the public, but she also declared that
she would never stoop to satisfy the public
taste, had she to leave those regions of
'purity of composition' in which she

soared. She affected much literary taste, endeavoured to gather round her a literary throng such as has filled the rooms of Maria Edgeworth, or Letitia Landon, or Jane Austen. But she did not succeed; she managed to get together a few weak authors and authoresses who had written reams of poetry—sold afterwards by the pound—and novels without originality or thought, and this is the circle in which she moved. Her ladyship's life languished in sighing to become what she never could be—an authoress, and in endeavouring to gather round her people who always refused her invitations. Her husband bore with all this very well, because his wife added dignity to his position; but he was ever regretting that he had no son and heir.

Lady Isabelle was pleased with the appearance of Patrick O'Leary. She expected to find in him a rough unsophisticated young man from the country, but she saw the reverse. She had heard that he was no gentleman by birth, but she found him a gentleman in manners. And so Patrick O'Leary often passed the evening at 'Arden,' as her ladyship's residence was called, and was introduced to her friends as the celebrated violinist.

He took a fancy to Lady Isabelle, although she sometimes took it into her head to read aloud to Patrick passages from her books, because she said that if he listened carefully he would gather ideas for musical compositions, and probably schemes on which to base concertos, which would surpass in grandeur and originality anything he had yet composed.

In originality most certainly, if a concerto were based upon the following :

' Lady Monkton grew faintly weary at the trysting-place. She was clad in mouse-colour trimmed with pale cerise; she looked like a dream, like a beautiful frail amethyst thing that could be shattered at the breath of a wood-sylph or at the glance of an ardent faun. Her bosom rose and fell beneath the delicate cambric kerchief, less snowy than her fair skin. " He cometh not," she muttered in agitation, which she tried to restore with her delicately perfumed vinaigrette. But it was in vain ; her thoughts were wild, wilder than the snowy winds of March, and the wind bore away upon its bosom the scent of the white rose, for that was the perfume in her vinaigrette. It was borne through the woods by the evening land-breeze, out, out to sea ; and then the mariner would say, as he lay upon a coil of rope smoking his pipe, ' Is this the breath from some orange-grove-skirted shore, or a kiss from Paradise?"'

But there was an element at Kingsborough which called forth Pat's music to a greater degree than Lady Isabelle's soirées and effusions of prose, and this element was the sea. Pat would sit by it for hours together, and would compose wilder, weirder strains than even he had composed in Inchigeela days. And then again it would soothe and hush his nature, which would find its companion in quiet, almost devotional strains.

There is something so sad in the fall of the sea, in the monotony of its thud and of its sigh, whether you sit by its shore or lie awake and listen to it in the night.

It is never weary; it comes endlessly to the shore, be it calm or rough. It is a fit example of life in its restlessness, and a fit emblem of heaven in its calm repose when it lies without a ripple on a summer's day; and when it comes roaring to the shore in the majesty of wildness, it speaks of the might and mystery of God. It is like music; the sound of sweet music and of the waves upon the shore have the same effect upon a mind that is capable of feeling. The one and the other call forth the noblest parts of mind in strains of thought; recollections crowd upon him who listens to music heard once before, long ago, with one who is no longer by; and so does the past rush upon him who stands upon the pebbly beach or tawny sand and listens to the beating of the sad waves as they give a long-drawn sigh as of relief that their rolling and tossing is over, and merge the end of their existence into those that follow after them. So may it be with us! May those who follow catch our latest breath, which speaks of rest found on a happier shore; may they follow us to the same sunny coast and join us there, while, in their turn, they leave encouragement and example to those who come after, and the breath that will speak of the ending of trouble and worldly struggles, and of that peace which is the reward of a well-fought earthly life.

CHAPTER X.

CONCLUSION.

'Farewell, a word that must be.'

FIFTEEN years have passed away; Mr. and Mrs. Frank Clavering are as happy as they were on the day of their marriage. There is no change in their hearts; they are both certain that they are the happiest pair in the world—except for one great sorrow, and that touches them both: Frank's father has passed away from them. He died quite suddenly at 'The Glen.' One morning he had been romping with his grandchildren before breakfast, as was his wont. He seemed well enough at breakfast, but afterwards lay down upon a sofa, and passed away as though in sleep.

His death was a great blow to all. His grandchildren missed him terribly. He had never wearied of playing with them, or of reading to them, or of telling them stories of long long ago, when he was a little boy, or of the time when he served his king and country. He entered into their games, into their little joys and sorrows, as though he were their own age.

He taught them to fence, and to ride like young Nimrods. When he left them for a time, their spirits seemed to forsake them ; and when he was called from among them for good, a blight fell upon them.

It was their first sorrow, but it was a deep one.

Mr. and Mrs. Francis Clavering were, as they said, an old married couple. At any rate their children, who were big for their age, made them seem so.

Kathleen often recalled the time when she was fickle and did not know her own mind, when she thought in moments. And she compared that time with this, and drew comparisons between fancy and love, which were not at all in favour of the former.

Ah, fancy, foolish fancy! the charm of an hour, the infatuation of a moment, without depth or consideration, without knowledge or foresight on the woman's part, without all that is worthy on the man's side. With the woman it is his handsome captivating manner; with the man it is the passion of a fleeting season, the admiration of a pretty face; it is all nothing, nothing more than the bloom on the plum, or the gold on the butterfly's wing, or the pollen on the yellow stamen of the virgin-white lily.

And what a contrast to this is pure love, the love that is as warm in the wintry weather of sorrow and want, as in the sunny days of joy and plenty! The love that increases with years, and goes down the hill as deeply and as truly as in its early life!

> ' Oh love for a week, a year, a day ;
> But alas for the love that will love alway !'

The love of a moment, of a year, of 'the cupboard,' is as plentiful as sand upon the seashore, as the poppies in a corn-field;

but the love of years is a far scarcer human gift or acquirement. Yes, *acquirement;* how much will a little self-denial on the part of a young husband or wife strengthen a love which may begin well and warmly, and how much it will go towards cementing two hearts together! How much a little yielding, a little sympathy will do! And if the opposite system be adopted, love will grow cold, and the selfishness of the one and the selfishness of the other will blossom into briars instead of into myrtle-trees.

What a holy sight it is to see an aged couple living a completely unselfish life, each one of them wrapped up in the wants of the other! Their love has been exactly the same in all seasons and through all changes; worldly losses have not estranged them, sorrows have not weakened their

42—2

affection ; but the reverses of life, whatever and no matter how many they may have been, have knit them closer and closer together.   They look forward to no separation in death ; the word 'separation' has no meaning for them ; they rather look beyond the grave, beyond the black and turbid waters of death's dark narrow stream, to where the heavenly dawn is breaking, and to where, once more reunited, they shall live in the confidence that where they are there can be no separation, and no more sorrow.

Mr. Clavering left all his property to his son, except a provision for his *protégé.*

No one could possibly have mourned more deeply over a benefactor's death, than did Pat O'Leary over the death of his friend and patron.   For a time he was perfectly inconsolable. All that Frank and Kathleen and their children could say and do was useless. He would not touch his violin; they asked him again and again to play favourite airs which their father and grandfather had loved, but he sullenly refused. In fact he shut himself up in his own room, and would not even admit the sunlight. The world seemed no longer the same to him; his whole interest in music appeared to depart for the time being, his existence had lost its object, and he mourned as those who are without hope.

For some months all endeavours to raise Pat's spirits were useless. His music might alone have restored him, but he really feared lest the strains of his violin would revive more than anything else the memory of his departed friend, and would recall to his mind those circumstances of his life in which Mr. Clavering had played not only a prominent part, but the part of a most affectionate friend. But by-and-by time toned and mellowed his grief, and he took to his music with greater vigour and enthusiasm than ever. He had risen to great eminence as a violin-player, and made his music his profession, in spite of what Mr. Clavering had said to the contrary long before.

His engagements were very numerous, and a high price was paid for his musical services in public and in private. But besides his manual dexterity on his violin, he set his head to work more than ever, and composed many concertos. Their originality was great, although not based upon passages from Lady Isabelle's novels. They were noted for purity of composition and for their exquisite finish and delicacy.

There was much that was weird in them, but also much that was most pathetic, almost heart-rending; and in everything that he composed there was an echo of the music which he used to play in the woods at Inchigeela long ago.

More particularly was this noticeable in a concerto which he christened 'Les Feuilles;' or rather he himself called it 'The Leaves,' but one who knew the public taste suggested a French rendering as more likely to go down.

It was a remarkable composition, certainly, and intended to represent the four seasons: the bursting of the buds in spring; the dancing and flickering of the leaves in summer; the wild bustle of dying and dead leaves in autumn, whirled hither and thither by loud winds; and the sigh of sorrow at the barrenness of winter, and a sob for the year that was fled. And in the autumn music there was much that resembled the music of the days when the blind boy spent hours of the night in the woods or in the fields, with his hat thrown aside, while the wind played with his fair hair and seemed to him like the fingers of God. His music was born with him, and that is why there was so much nature in it.

The praises of people never turned his head; he always maintained great simplicity and humility of manner. Half or a quarter of the praise he did receive, would have turned the head of many a wiser and stronger man than Pat O'Leary. He was petted in society, had presents and smiles and compliments without end bestowed upon him; but he never would allow that he was worthy of praise. If he had genius it was not his own giving or his own making, but the possession of it should make him humble, and grateful to the Great Source from whence 'cometh down every good and perfect gift.'

As to his domestic life, the musician lived and married happily; and with this assurance we must be content to leave him, though we would fain follow him farther.

He never forgot his good benefactor, but held him up as an example of piety and love to his children.

Frank and Kathleen lived to a good old age in the enjoyment of a happy home, tended and loved by their children and grandchildren ; and when they died, each of them looked forward to an eternal union.

An attempt has been made to depict some of the virtues and vices, as well as some of the beauties and wretchednesses, of human nature.   Sorrow has been painted, so has joy ; valour and truth, as well as cowardice and falsehood ; warm-hearted charity and devotion, as well as selfishness and coldness of heart ; unreality and pretentiousness, as opposed to reality and sterling worth.

If the colouring has been shallow, and the design poor, forgive, gentle reader, the shortcomings of the author, who trusts that, in spite of great inefficiency on his part, you may have beguiled a weary hour with his book, and may have carried away some lesson which, however small, may find a profitable result in the life you are leading and in the goal you are aiming at.

THE END.

BILLING AND SONS, PRINTERS, GUILDFORD, SURREY.

Lightning Source UK Ltd.
Milton Keynes UK
UKHW052354191118
332601UK00007B/567/P